CRIME TRAVELERS

BOOK 2

DIAMONDS ARE FOR NEVER

An International Adventure Novel
Featuring Lucas Benes and the NEW RESISTANCE

PAUL AERTKER

FLYING SOLO PRESS

ROME | SEATTLE | LONDON | NEW YORK | PARIS | DENVER

HONG KONG | CAPE TOWN | LOS ANGELES | SAN JOSE

Library Meta Data

Aertker, Paul

Crime Travelers / Paul Aertker.— 1st ed.

p. 256 cm. 12.7 x 20.32 (5x8 in) — (Diamonds Are For Never ; bk. 2)

Summary: After sabotaging a mass kidnapping in Paris, Lucas Benes
faces a new and perilous threat from Siba Günerro and her anything-but-good
Good Company.

When a briefcase-toting kid from the Falkland Islands joins the New Resistance,
Lucas learns the truth about his mother and becomes a boy on a mission.

Lucas and friends speed in and around Rome—from the Colosseum to the
Vatican—until they stow away on a cargo ship carrying diamonds that could
unlock the secret to Lucas's past and destroy the Good Company's future.

In this action-packed second installment of the Crime Travelers series, author
Paul Aertker takes readers on a gripping world tour filled with adrenaline, humor,
and pure excitement. © 2015, FSP

1. Travel—Fiction. 2. Language and languages—Fiction. 3. Conspiracies—
Fiction. 4. Cargo Ships—Fiction. 5. Diamonds—Fiction. 6. Geography—
Fiction. 7. Multicultural—Fiction. 8. Europe—Fiction. 9. Rome, Italy—Fiction.
10. Pirates—Fiction.
1. Title. Pro 2015

Edited by Brian Luster using the Chicago Manual of Style, 16th edition
Cover Design by Pintado | Maps by Paul Devine | Interior Design by Amy
McKnight | All designs, maps, graphics, photographs © 2015 Paul Aertker and
Flying Solo Press, LLC

ISBN 978-1-940137-25-4 / eISBN 978-1-940137-26-1
Diamonds Are For Never | Printed worldwide
Library of Congress Control Number: 2015903582
US Copyright Registration Number: TX 8-412-778

To Larry Yoder

Thanks for believing in me and my books.

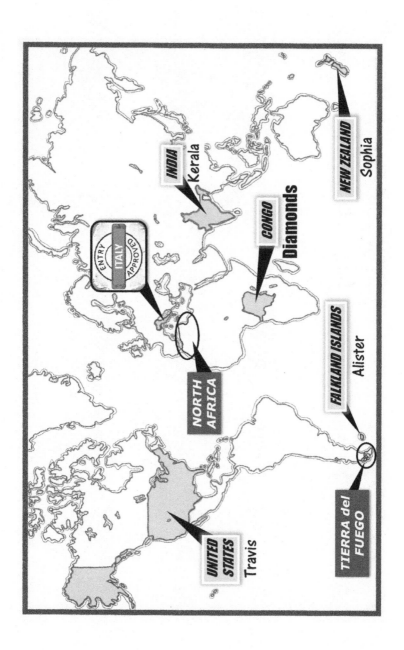

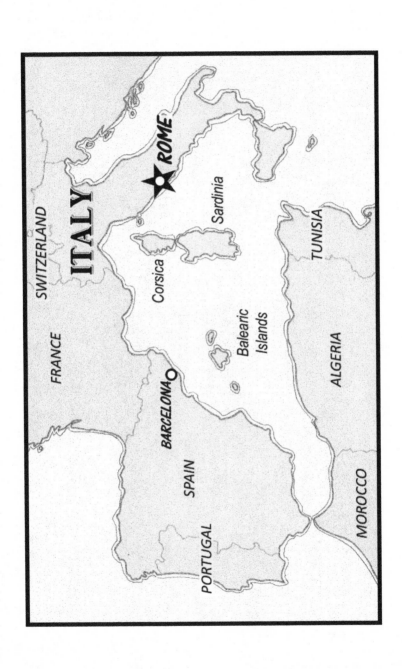

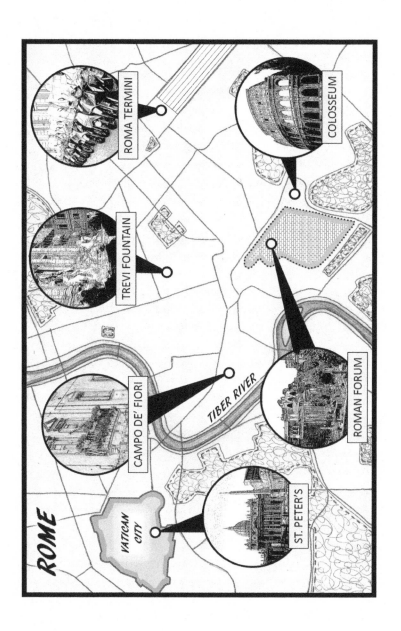

NEW RESISTANCE NOTEBOOK

CONGO (DRC)
CAPITAL
Kinshasa

LANGUAGE
French / Lingala / Swahili

POPULATION
77,000,000

AREA
2,300,000 sq km

NOTES
Diamond mines

NEW ZEALAND
CAPITAL
Wellington

LANGUAGE
English / Māori

POPULATION
5,000,000

AREA
300,000 sq km

NOTES
Sophia was born here

FALKLANDS
CAPITAL
Stanley

LANGUAGE
English

POPULATION
3,000

AREA
12,000 sq km

NOTES
Alister is from here

NORTH AFRICA
COUNTRIES
Morocco, Algeria, Tunisia

AREA
Borders southern Mediterranean Sea

NOTES
An area of Curukian recruitment for Ms. Gunerro and the Good Company

INDIA
CAPITAL
New Delhi

LANGUAGE
Hindi / English

POPULATION
1,210,000,000

AREA
3,300,000 sq km

NOTES
Kerala was born here

TIERRA del FUEGO
COUNTRIES
Chile, Argentina

AREA
Forms the southern tip of South America

NOTES
The meeting on the boat took place here

ITALY
CAPITAL
Rome

LANGUAGE
Italian

POPULATION
61,000,000

AREA
300,000 sq km

NOTES
Action Destination

UNITED STATES
CAPITAL
Washington, D.C.

LANGUAGE
English

POPULATION
320,000,000

AREA
9,100,000 sq km

NOTES
Ms. Gunerro is filming in California

CONTENTS

Your past doesn't have to define your future.

ANTARCTICA

With a pair of cat-eye goggles stretched across her eyes, Ms. Siba Günerro looked out over the bow of her ship.

The president and CEO of the Good Company gripped the railing as the largest vessel in the Good Company fleet, the *Lollipop*, sliced through the icy waters off Tierra del Fuego. The boat powered through the Bay of Good Success and rounded the tip of South America.

Seagulls squawked in the haze as they trailed the ship into international waters. Some four hundred nautical miles north of the tail of Antarctica the fog thinned, exposing small slabs of snowy floe that drifted like tiny white islands.

Dead ahead, a rogue iceberg bobbed its massive crown over the horizon. The glacial mass was so big that it looked like a section of Manhattan frozen over, with skyscrapers made of ice.

As they approached the floating mountain, the captain turned the ship to avoid the hidden under-side of the berg. A rumbling sound beat across the wide expanse of water. From behind the snow-white walls a matte-black Sikorsky helicopter thundered into view.

Shards of sleet swirled in a cone as the helicopter rose above the iceberg. The Sikorsky banked in a wide curve through the mist. Penguins, by the thousands, whistled as they slid from the ice into the sea. Strobe lights stabbed at the sky while searchlights crisscrossed the boat, guiding the helicopter through the fog.

Four boys in black jackets scurried across the *Lollipop*'s deck to the stern. With wand flashlights they directed the Sikorsky down to the landing pad. The side door popped open, and a block of steel steps unfolded to the platform.

A man scrambled out and ducked underneath the spinning blades.

Charles Magnus, head of Good Company Security, tossed a large parka to another man still in the helicopter. Magnus trotted forward to the bow to greet Ms. Günerro while the other man suited up. In the fifteen seconds it took to get to his boss, Magnus's breath had already started to freeze his thick beard.

Ms. Günerro spoke over the sound of the howling wind and ocean spray. "How was your trip to Tierra del Fuego?"

"Not much *fuego*," said Magnus, raising his voice. "It's freezing. If you haven't noticed."

Her eyes cut a quick but serious glance. "What did you find?"

Magnus zipped his coat all the way up to his throat. "I've reconfirmed the boy's identity," he said. "His full name is Lucas Kapriss Benes."

"How did you find that out?"

"Like you always say," Magnus said, "nuns are weak. They will always tell the truth."

"Nuns have to tell the truth," said Ms. Günerro, cackling. "Did you get the boy's birth chart?"

"That was a problem."

"What do you mean?"

"His birth chart is missing."

Ms. Günerro was silent. Magnus looked back and saw the other man climbing out of the helicopter. Then he turned back to his boss and dropped his eyes.

"The whole file has been missing since the morning of the ferryboat accident."

"I knew it," said Ms. Günerro. "That means Kate Benes stole it, and that means the bank account information must be in Lucas's birth chart. It's the only reason she would have taken it."

"Now what?"

"The next question is," said Ms. Günerro, "did the birth chart in fact go with Lucas in that ice chest?"

"If it did"—Magnus paused—"then Lucas Benes is a millionaire."

Ms. Günerro shook her head. "Don't be a fool, Chuckie. That was twelve years ago, and the international markets have been wild ever since. And remember, Bunguu paid us, *prepaid* us, in stocks, bonds, diamonds, gold, even ivory, and cash currencies from nearly every country." She paused. "If Lucas Benes has access to those accounts, he would be *not* a millionaire, but a *billionaire*."

"But he must not know it," said Magnus.

Ms. Günerro said, "Frankly, I don't think anyone at the New Resistance knows the truth."

On the roof of the ship's pilothouse, satellite dishes were spinning northward. A foursome of mustached boys in black jackets policed the boat's perimeter with giant ice picks.

A deckhand closed the helicopter's door.

Ms. Günerro's eyes sharpened on the man walking from the helicopter. "Does Bunguu know about what happened in Paris?"

"Yes, he knows," said Magnus.

Siba Günerro and Charles Magnus stared at each other with the same worried look. For them, this was a business trip. It was supposed to be the most profitable venture ever for the Good Company.

Supposed to be.

The Good Ship *Lollipop* was large enough to accommodate one hundred forty-eight passengers. The crew often liked to double-bunk kids like slaves and pack them in. But on this day the ship's cargo, some thirty-three children, was a fraction of its capacity because Lucas Benes and the New Resistance had foiled a Good Company kidnapping in Paris. And in doing so, they had cost Siba Günerro a fortune. Literally.

"Ah," said Ms. Günerro, grinning brightly. "*Mister* Bunguu.*"

Lu Bunguu walked hunched over as gusts of frigid wind slapped him in the face. Specks of white ice dotted his dark pores. The African-Asian man with long fingers yanked the hood of his parka around his face. He snarled at Ms. Günerro, showing his piano-key teeth.

Ms. Günerro extended her hand. "Welcome to paradise."

"Antarctica is not *parad*-ice, madam," said Bunguu. "It's just *plain* ice."

"It's absolutely *wunderbar*," said Ms. Günerro. "Absolutely wonderful."

Bunguu nodded impatiently. "The pilot said we must go soon. Nothing flies well in the Antarctic winter."

"It's a helicopter," said Ms. Günerro. "You'll be fine."

"At these temperatures," said Bunguu, his voice deep but respectful, "everything is disagreeable."

"The lack of ozone," said Ms. Günerro, "makes everything perfectly clear."

"I don't know about this ozone," said Bunguu. "I do know that it is a miserably cold place to have a meeting."

"It's heaven on earth," said Ms. Günerro, extending

her arms.

"Heaven?" Bunguu said with a look of shock on his face. "Antarctica?"

"Yes. If Hades is hot," Ms. Günerro said, "then heaven must be cold!"

Lu Bunguu stomped his foot on the deck. "Madam, we don't have time for such chatter!" He shivered. "I know you botched the kidnappings in Paris."

"It's just a glitch," said Ms. Günerro. "You know who and his group got in the way."

"John Beans?" said Bunguu.

Magnus corrected him. "It's Benes," he said. "It rhymes with *tennis*."

"Anywho," said Ms. Günerro. "Yes, Benes is making a fortune now from his chain of Globe Hotels and is pouring every cent into helping children, which is stopping us from doing our Good work."

Lu Bunguu shook his head. "The fact remains, madam, that I have already paid you for a product that you now seem unable to supply."

"We've consistently delivered children to you for years, Lu. Once I take care of the Benes problem, it'll be smooth sailing again."

"I don't think you understand," Bunguu said. "The problem is that for years we had a perfect supply of children for all kinds of work. But for the past twelve months you've delivered no one. We have open orders for hundreds of child soldiers in the Congo, in Ituri, Darfur, still in Rwanda, and Burundi, too."

"I'm aware of your labor shortage," Ms. Günerro said. "Children who work as soldiers quite often die and must be replaced."

Mr. Bunguu eyed Ms. Günerro. "There is another matter."

"What?" asked Magnus.

"Word on the street," Bunguu said, "is that the Good Company has lost access to those secret funds that I paid you twelve years ago."

"Nonsense!" said Ms. Günerro with a weak chuckle. "My Good Hotels are making us millions every night of the year. I have kept the diamonds and gold you paid us a secret because it *is* a secret. If the bankers in North America and Europe find out that I have hidden bank accounts, they will stick their noses in everything we do."

"You have meetings in Antarctica in winter," said Bunguu. "Neither of you knows anything!"

Ms. Günerro huffed. "Mr. Bunguu—"

"I knew twelve years ago you'd lost that money," Bunguu said, gritting his teeth. "I've been trying to find it ever since. But I just learned that there is a banker in the Falklands who's been asking about the container of money.

"So yes," said Bunguu. "You're a liar and you owe me and you will repay me. Is that clear?"

"Come now, Lu," Ms. Günerro said. "We're old friends."

"Old as in finished," said Bunguu. "I will give you

two choices. Within the next year, you will either return my money or its equivalent, or deliver five hundred children to me for each of the next twelve months."

"Are you serious?" said Ms. Günerro.

Bunguu nodded and pulled his coat tight around his chest.

"And if we don't?" Magnus asked.

Bunguu turned toward the helicopter. "Then the governments in America and Europe will find out about your hidden accounts, the child trafficking, and your other *good* activities. And those governments will freeze the money from all your Good Hotels.

"And, madam," he continued, "don't think for a moment that they will ever discover a relationship between you and me."

Lu Bunguu marched headlong to the helicopter. He climbed in and slammed the door closed behind him. From the window Bunguu glared at Ms. Günerro and Magnus. The Sikorsky's engine whirred as the helicopter lifted off the landing pad. The pilot turned north toward Cape Horn, gliding out over the water.

Ms. Günerro watched Bunguu fly away. Then she grinned and let out a cackle that seemed to spread out across the bottom of the planet.

"Magnus!" she snapped.

"Yes."

"I want you to fly to Buenos Aires," Ms. Günerro said.

"Why?"

"Because we need a mother from Argentina."

"But *his* mother is—"

"I know what happened," Ms. Günerro said. "But Lucas doesn't, and he will always look for her." She paused. "Get the mother and the boy will follow her. Follow the boy and we'll get the money."

MONEY CAN BUY THE BEST FRIENDS

At the Good Hotel Buenos Aires, Argentina, a New Resistance waiter attached a GoPro to his tray and started filming.

Charles Magnus marched through the front doors of the hotel and stopped beneath the glass chandelier in the middle of the lobby, where he met a dark-haired woman dressed in a blue police uniform. Her name was Charlotte Janssens, and she was an agent with Interpol, the International Criminal Police Organization, which assisted with police cooperation across the globe.

They shook hands and walked to the lobby café, where they sat at a table and ordered two coffees from the waiter.

The Interpol agent spoke English with a clean, international accent.

"Good morning," she said.

"Hello, Charlotte," Magnus said. "How was your trip from France?"

"Long. How was your trip from Tierra del Fuego?"

"Cold," Magnus said. He glanced around the lobby to make sure no one was spying on them. "Do you have the information we're looking for?"

From her jacket pocket Agent Janssens removed a small box with the word EVIDENCE written on the outside. She slid it across the table.

Magnus palmed the box and looked back toward the front doors. Guests dressed for a cold day were streaming in and out of the hotel. Magnus turned back and took the top off the box. Inside he found a large diamond. He picked it up and rolled it between his fingers.

"Where did you find this?"

"This particular diamond was found on a dock just outside of Rome."

"Italy?"

"The one and only."

"How do you know this is one of the diamonds we're looking for?"

"First of all," Agent Janssens said, "I am the Interpol special agent in charge of diamond theft worldwide. I know diamonds. Secondly, this is the fifth such gem we've found in the last two months. Two mysteriously showed up on the shipping docks in Australia and Indonesia. More were spotted in Dubai and Turkey. Then, earlier this week, this one was found in Civitavecchia northwest of Rome. And lastly, I have not seen a diamond cut like this since the Kapriss diamonds."

Magnus pulled an envelope from his jacket pocket and handed it to Agent Janssens. She peeked in and saw hundreds of American one-hundred-dollar bills.

CHAPTER TWO

"What about the diamond?" she asked.

"You keep it," he said, handing it to her. "If your information is correct, then we'll have plenty more for the Good Company."

"Thank you," she said. "But I've only given you partial information. I don't know which container the diamonds are in or on which ship."

"That's okay, we know where the container is now," he said. "And the boy will tell us the rest."

"And how do you know he'll take the bait?"

"In two days, I'll have some Curukians at his hotel in Las Vegas. They'll plant a seed that the boy can't resist."

Agent Janssens nodded. "For a backup plan, I'll put him in our database as wanted for questioning. What's his full name again?"

"Lucas Kapriss Benes."

"Interesting."

The waiter returned to the table with two cups. Magnus smiled as he slurped his coffee.

A STRANGE FLASH OF COLD

Charles Magnus said good-bye to Agent Janssens and left the café in the Good Hotel Buenos Aires.

He marched across the lobby and spoke to the concierge. The man behind the desk nodded and picked up his phone. Magnus then walked past the reservations desk, and without stopping, he headed straight into the housekeeping office.

Fifteen minutes later he and a woman with long black hair left the room. They exited the hotel through a back door and got into a waiting hotel van.

The driver took them out of the alley, turned right, and headed into town. They passed the presidential palace, the Casa Rosada, where Evita Perón gave her famous "Don't Cry for Me, Argentina" speech. Outside the Cabildo, the old town hall, a line of soldiers marched in red-white-and-blue uniforms. The driver took Magnus and his guest thirty-five kilometers southwest of downtown through heavy traffic to the Ezeiza International Airport.

Magnus opened the passenger door and stepped out with a leather satchel draped over his shoulder. He opened the side door to let the woman out.

Police officers directed traffic with ear-piercing whistles, and the air smelled of jet fuel. Magnus offered the woman a hand, and they walked into the airport, where they picked up tickets at the Copa Airlines counter. They checked no bags. They proceeded through the airport past several restaurants, information booths, and duty-free shops.

After security, they headed to gate number three on the international concourse. Three hours later they boarded a flight for Panama, where they changed planes. They sat in first class. On the second flight they ate steak and lentils for dinner, and after coffee, the woman fell asleep. Magnus stayed awake.

The flight attendant's voice came over the PA system.

He said, "Ladies and gentlemen, as we begin our descent, please make sure your seat backs and tray tables are in their full upright and uncomfortable position. We'll be landing in Las Vegas in a few minutes."

For the first time on the flight Magnus and the woman spoke.

Magnus asked, "You do know why we're here, don't you?"

"Yes," the woman said, "we're going to a hotel conference. And I'm going to be made head of housekeeping at the Good Hotels in America."

"That's partly true," Magnus said. "But Ms. Günerro has one more test for you."

The woman wrinkled an eyebrow.

Magnus rubbed his beard. "It's an acting job."

"What do you mean?" said the woman with long black hair. "I'm not an actor."

The passengers began taking their carry-on bags down from the overhead bins. When it came time for the woman with long black hair to get up, Magnus stood first and took a white binder from his satchel.

"Everything you need to know," he said, handing her the file, "is in here." He leaned across the seat. "Read everything in this handbook. And memorize it. And then destroy it."

"Then what?"

"You play your part," he said. He grinned under his beard. "And you will meet someone who thinks he knows you. A boy."

"And if I don't go along?"

"Do you remember Luz Kapriss?"

"Of course I remember Luz," she said. "Everyone knows what Ms. T did to her."

"T didn't do anything except take her on a boat ride."

"And Luz never came back."

"Luz was a free spirit," Magnus said. "She wanted to see the world. But like Icarus, she flew too close to the sun and got burned."

"That's not what I heard."

"You can either follow the plan," Magnus whispered, "or you can take a boat ride with Ms. T."

The woman with long black hair winced in fear

and bowed her head like she was trying to curl up and disappear. She closed her eyes and breathed deeply.

"And you know exactly where he is?" she asked.

"I have Lucas's room number."

"How did you get that?"

"I have friends on the inside."

"So," she asked, "how will I know when it's over?"

"It's over when we have the codes and the information from the boy's file."

Half an hour later the woman with long black hair left the airport and hailed a taxi to take her to the Good Hotel Las Vegas. As she walked in the Nevadan heat, she felt a strange flash of cold.

A BODY IN MOTION

Lucas Benes woke in a cold sweat.

Lying in his sleeping bag on the roof of his father's hotel, Lucas felt connected, somehow tethered to another world, another life. He focused on the cloudless Nevada sky and tried to remember what he had seen in his sleep.

Dreams always seemed to fade as quickly as they came, leaving behind only fragments. Lucas figured his mind must be jumbling fiction and reality.

He wasn't sure what to make of the dream.

At hotel-school there were old arguments about the meaning of dreams. Ms. Dodge, the science teacher, called dreams "nighttime cerebral visions." She said they were a way for the body to flush out the unused information in the brain. Lucas's English teacher, Dr. Sherman, differed. He said that dreams were a form of time travel, which helped you make sense of the here and now.

Lucas preferred Dr. Sherman's version.

Sleep slowly came again, and Lucas traveled back in his mind. He drifted into picturing his most recent "nighttime vision." He felt like he was remembering what had happened to him when he was a baby at the Good Hospital in Tierra del Fuego. There had been icebergs in the sea off Tierra del Fuego, but he hadn't been there since he was two—when the ferryboat accident nearly killed him.

Half-awake, half-asleep, Lucas flipped through the details in his memory. Kate Benes had only been his mother for a day. She had gone to southern Argentina to adopt him and some other babies from the nuns at the Good Hospital. She had saved his life by putting him in an ice chest just before their boat hit a freak iceberg.

And then the boat exploded.

So Lucas technically had had two mothers before he turned two years old. His adoptive mother and his birth mother. Both were now dead, which was why he could only dream about them.

But Ms. Günerro had promised that his birth mother was alive.

Part of Lucas knew it was a lie. On the surface this news couldn't be true. It just wasn't logical. Still, somewhere in his heart there was a tiny sprig of hope that his birth mother was alive. Just maybe.

He sat up, patted down his bed-head hair, and looked around the rooftop. As usual he was alone, which was why he slept on the roof in the first place. To get away from the drama of the Globe Hotel and the New Resistance Hotel-School. Slowly his brain filled with data.

It was the first day of school for the new term. Lucas secretly wanted some great tragedy to happen, some awful storm that would cancel school for days. The Globe Hotel was located in the desert, in Nevada—a Spanish word that meant "snow covered."

The irony was not funny to Lucas. There was definitely no chance of a snow day. Not in Las Vegas. Not on August first.

Six weeks earlier he'd dreamed about his mother and had found a baby lying in a shopping cart in the back parking lot. Lucas flung open the already unzipped sleeping bag and peered over the concrete wall.

This particular morning was turning out to be equally as odd. At that very moment a bowling ball began rolling across the asphalt. The heavy ball crunched across the loose grit and gravel and rolled into a pile of construction sand, where it made an indentation and stopped.

Weird, Lucas thought.

He scanned the back parking lot to see where the ball had come from. Surely it had been left over from the van that had picked him up six weeks ago and spilled Busball balls all over the place.

Newton's laws of physics flashed in Lucas's brain. A body (or a bowling ball, in this case) at rest will stay at rest unless acted upon by an external force. It had to be a person. Someone was in the back parking lot.

Maybe, Lucas thought, *it's the guys I met in June.*

The Curukians who were helping me and the New Resistance.

Lucas's internal clock told him he was already late for breakfast. As he was stowing his sleeping bag, he heard the stairwell door to the roof crash open. A pair of sandals slapped across the rooftop.

Holding a hairbrush, his fourteen-year-old sister, Astrid, called out, "Put on some clothes, would you, please?"

"I'm getting dressed," Lucas said, picking up a pair of sport shorts.

"Are you wearing boxers?" Astrid asked. "You wear boxers to bed?"

"Uh, yeah," said Lucas. "I'm fourteen. What do you expect me to wear to bed? Pajamas? Turn around!"

Astrid faced the other way and brushed her hair while Lucas put on the shorts and a T-shirt.

"Are you finished yet?" Astrid asked.

"Yeah, yeah," said Lucas. "I just had the weirdest dream, but it made me remember my mother. It's hard to believe she might be alive."

"We know, Lucas," Astrid said, running the brush through her hair again. "You've been talking about Ms. Günerro telling you about your mother being alive for a month and a half now."

"I have not."

"Did you write your summer essay on it?" Astrid said.

"Yeah, sure."

"You're lying," she said. "And not to be harsh, but so is Ms. Günerro."

Lucas's mind populated with a cast of characters and places from Paris: the Good Company, a French kid named Hervé, the Shakespeare and Company bookshop. Jackknife and Travis in the Notre Dame Cathedral at Ms. Günerro's weird brainwashing ceremony. He remembered Charles Magnus on a motorcycle, chasing him through the streets of Paris. And the Curukians—Siba Günerro's boys who would do anything she asked.

Lucas rolled up his foam mattress and stowed it with the sleeping bag in the plastic bin he kept for himself on the roof.

"Hey, Astrid," he said. "Where's Gini?"

"Dad's worried about her," Astrid said. "So Nalini's taking care of her now."

"Why?"

"Apparently," Astrid said, "someone broke into the nurse's office at the Globe Hotel and stole some birth charts and then tossed them in the dumpster."

"Who would do that?"

"We don't know." Astrid turned to leave. "Coach Creed sent me up here to get you," she said. "The next term is about to start and the new kids are coming this morning. That means you get a roommate."

"I thought they were going to live in the dorms downstairs."

"They are," Astrid said, "when the dorms are

finished. But there's something wrong with the concrete or something like that. So until then you have to share a room."

"I don't want a roommate," Lucas said. "I'm kind of tired of everybody."

"Yeah, me too," said Astrid. "Well anyway, the hall monitors are moving the girls to the eighth floor and the boys to the seventh floor. You're going to be late if you don't hurry."

"I know," said Lucas.

"You don't wear a watch or know where your phone is," she said. "How do you know what time it is?"

"I have a clock in my head."

"What time is it?"

"Seven oh three."

Astrid glanced at her phone. She turned it so Lucas could see. It said 7:02, and then it changed to 7:03.

"I'll be right there," Lucas said as Astrid headed into the stairwell.

Yeah, he thought. *As soon as I find out who's signaling me with that bowling ball.*

CHAPTER 5

LET'S MAKE A DEAL

From the Globe Hotel roof, Lucas could smell coffee and hot chocolate coming through the kitchen vents. And doughnuts, too. They were classic combinations. But the sweet fried dough meant that it was the first day of class, and deep down Lucas just didn't want to go to school.

Ever.

Summer was never long enough.

Never.

The new school year didn't start for a whole nother fifty-seven minutes. Lucas figured he had plenty of time to find out who was in the parking lot.

Lucas looked over the wall again and eyed the bowling ball. He wondered if it wasn't a signal, but rather a trap. In Paris he had helped destroy part of the Good Company's kidnapping ring. Ms. Günerro would surely come after him, and she would send Curukians first. No doubt.

Lucas tamped down his self-doubt and prepared to rappel down. He stepped on the climbing platform, let out some line, and dropped. As he descended, he bounced off the exterior wall of the hotel. He sprang out three, four times and swung wide, like he was on a kite board. Lucas Benes had mastered the solo rappel.

Two minutes later he landed on the ground and eased around the side of the hotel. He couldn't hear much except for the jackhammering in the construction site below ground. Behind a lumber pile workers in hard hats loaded stones into a massive rock crusher.

Someone wrapped in a white Mexican serape cut between a stack of two-by-fours and then disappeared.

The laundry vents on the back of the hotel were blowing a sweet, clean smell into the air, and Lucas considered sneezing. But then he noticed that the bowling ball was now missing.

Lucas moved diagonally across the parking lot toward the dumpsters. He rounded the pile of sand and cut behind a stack of lumber. The workers he'd spotted earlier were nowhere to be found. Strangely, the rock crusher spun in a slow circle, chewing on bits of stone.

If someone wanted to meet him, Lucas reasoned that he should make himself available. He stepped around the lumber and now found himself boxed in by the dumpsters on one side and the rock crusher and a muddy area behind the basketball hoops on the other. A vulnerable spot. The hairs on the back of his neck rose up.

Sometimes being scared to death was better than being bored to death.

"Hello?" Lucas called out to no one he could see.

He heard footsteps. Two pairs of shoes.

Lucas spun around.

A bowling ball came flying straight at his chest. Lucas flapped his arms, jumped back, and let the ball bomb into the puddle of muddy water.

"What did you do that for?" Lucas asked as he slurped his shoe out of the mud.

"I heard you were quick," the tall boy said.

"You know me?"

"Are you Lucas Benes?" said the short boy.

Lucas sized up the two guys. They were definitely Curukians.

All-black clothing. Peach-fuzz mustaches. One tall. One not. The shorter one wore a muscle shirt.

They were perfect examples of the expression "birds of a feather flock together"—like they never even thought for themselves. Maybe that was what being brainwashed really was all about. People not thinking for themselves. There were so many like that. People who just did what others did and thought the way other people thought.

Brainwashed.

Lucas said, "Who wants to know?"

"Every Curukian in the world," said Tall Boy.

Lucas heard an Eastern European accent.

"So where are your accents from?" Lucas asked.

"Raffish, Curuk."

"Oh, right," said Lucas, reminding himself that Curukians said they were from the fictitious place made up of the initials of the five United Nations Security Council countries: the US, the UK, Russia, France, and China.

Both boys were twitching and fidgeting. When people were anxious, they normally did a bad job of hiding what they wanted.

In his mind Lucas could hear Coach Creed telling him to let the other guys make the first mistake. All Lucas had to do was hold on, and they would tell him everything he needed.

He waited a total of seven seconds.

"We heard about what you did in Paris," Muscle Shirt said.

"Ms. Günerro is meta mad," Tall Boy said. "You wrecked her bus."

"She told the cops," Muscle Shirt said, "and they're looking for you. Your name is all over Interpol."

Lucas could have argued with them about who really wrecked the bus, but that would serve no purpose. He could just as easily walk or run away. But Lucas wanted to know why they were visiting the Globe Hotel Las Vegas.

"Ms. Günerro has a bounty out for you," Tall Boy said.

"But we're here to make you a deal," said Muscle Shirt. "Your birth chart from Tierra del Fuego is missing, and Ms. Günerro believes there are some account numbers and codes in that file that will tell us where your mother hid the Good Company money."

This wasn't going to end well. Lucas knew as much.

Muscle Shirt said, "Before Ms. Günerro and Mr. Magnus find you, we thought we'd offer you an arrangement."

"You see," said the other boy, "if we get this chart with the numbers and codes before the other Curukians, then Ms. Günerro will reward us."

"And if you give it to us with no trouble," said Muscle Shirt, "then we'll split the reward with you. One third. One third. One third."

"How much is the bounty?"

Tall Boy glared. "What do you mean?"

"How much am I worth to Ms. Günerro and the Good Company?"

Muscle Shirt shrugged. "Three million bucks. US."

It was time to end the discussion.

"A million apiece?" Lucas asked. "That's all? I like to think that I'm worth a lot more than that."

Both boys seemed dumbfounded by Lucas's logic. But it pushed the conversation to its conclusion. In Lucas's experience when people wanted something and hadn't gotten what they wanted they would often resort to one of three things.

One, they would give you the silent treatment and walk away in a huff. Two, they would step up the monologue and pound you with insults or pleas—"Come on, come on." Or three, they would use force and try to scare it out of you.

Brainwashed Curukians have never been known

as great thinkers or philosophers or boys of higher learning. Fighting was a perfectly good option to them.

Lucas didn't want this, but he prepared to defend himself. He calmed his nerves and tightened his core. A human being, locked and loaded.

Tall Boy snatched the bowling ball from the mud and strutted to the other side of the two-by-fours. Cocky. Then, like he was playing basketball, he shot the heavy ball into the mouth of the rock crusher. The bowling ball rolled and clanked around the metal drum like a giant uncooked popcorn kernel.

"This is what's going to happen to you," Tall Boy said, "if you don't give us your birth chart."

A second later the cylinder's grinding teeth grabbed hold of the bowling ball, and the blades pulverized it. Bits of rock and dust spewed from the back of the machine.

Impressive, Lucas thought. *And wasteful, too.*

"Fellas," Lucas said, "I'm going to be late for school."

The boys grabbed Lucas by the arms and lifted him in the air.

Stupid move, Lucas thought.

His feet were now inches from their thighs. In one swift motion Lucas jabbed them in the legs, his rubber-bottomed climbing shoes scraping down their quads. Lucas pumped his feet and then stabbed his shoes into their kneecaps. The boys let go of Lucas, and the three of them spilled onto the ground.

Within seconds they were back on their feet. Lucas watched their dark eyes. He was looking for a sign, a cue from one to the other to signal the next attack. They would favor the injured knees and protect them. The boys kicked their loafers off and switched places. Tall Boy put his right foot forward, which meant he was probably left-footed and therefore left-handed.

Lucas adjusted his stance.

The boys leaned forward, then tilted backward. Tall Boy's left foot and Muscle Shirt's right foot moved upward. Lucas squatted to the ground like a catcher so that the boys' feet were above his head. The Curukians were now standing on only one foot each.

Two egrets—unbalanced and ready to fall.

Lucas grabbed the Achilles tendons on the boys' rising feet. Using their momentum, he stood up, raising the two boys' feet high in the air. In one swift and dull thud both Curukians crashed onto the pavement, smacking their skulls on the asphalt. Lucas scurried around the dumpster and stripped one of the plastic straps from the pile of two-by-fours.

In a matter of seconds he bound the boys' hands and tied them—through their crotches—to each other.

Lucas stepped back. He knew that he had to read his birth chart again and figure out what these guys were looking for, and why.

AN UNWELCOME GUEST

A shrill sound of an electric engine hummed in the distance and sent a chill up Lucas's spine.

The flatbed golf cart buzzed across the parking lot, its fat tires crunching through the construction sand. Lucas turned and saw Coach Creed with an unshaven face, driving like a crazy Texan. In the passenger seat was John Benes, Lucas's dad and CEO of the Globe Hotels.

Mr. Benes, dressed in a blue sport coat, hopped off the golf cart while it was still rolling. Coach Creed mashed a boot on the brake pedal and skidded the cart to a stop.

"What in the hay is going on here?" The Texan asked.

"They jumped me," Lucas said.

Behind a pair of rectangular glasses, John Benes's blue eyes scanned the scene.

Coach Creed moved straight to the two boys lying on the ground. He paused for a second, then knelt between them and touched their necks. Lucas figured he was checking their pulses to see if they were still alive. For a second Coach didn't say anything. Then he put his ear to the boys' chests. When he leaned forward, Coach's khaki pants sagged and exposed his Texas-sized butt crack, which was now pointing up to the sky.

"You boys are going to be fine," he declared. "You can stay in the infirmary with our new nurse for the next couple of days."

With a Swiss Army knife, Coach cut the straps that Lucas had used to tie the boys up. Then, without any difficulty, he scooped up Muscle Shirt and put him in the back of the golf cart.

"How did you know I was down here?" Lucas asked.

"Astrid watched you from the roof," Mr. Benes said. "She called us."

Coach glanced at Lucas. "What did they want?" he asked.

"My birth chart."

"That can't be," Coach said as he stood over Tall Boy. "Why not?"

"Lucas," Mr. Benes said, "we've all been over your birth file a hundred times in the last six weeks and we can't find anything that makes sense. You've seen it for yourself."

Lucas knew in his heart that there was a message there in his birth file. "When I was on the bus with Ms. Günerro in Paris, all she wanted was some stupid account number. She wanted to know what they put with me in the ice chest that saved my life. And all I had was a bell and my birth chart. It *has* to be important. It has to be."

"I'm sure it's very important," Coach said as he put Tall Boy in the cart with Muscle Shirt. "But your mother used codes that don't seem to make sense to anyone."

"Coach is right, Lucas," Mr. Benes said. "Your birth file is littered with cryptic doctor scribble and meaningless numbers and letters. Maybe the codes meant something to your mother, but to us, it's nonsense."

"I want to look at the file again."

"That's not going to happen," Mr. Benes said. "If there is information in your file, then I don't want it to get into Günerro's hands. I had the locks on the file room changed this morning. No one is getting in there. No one."

Coach Creed plopped into the driver's seat of the golf cart. He clicked the pedal and waved his hand in the air. The cart whined around the side of the hotel and out of sight.

"Let's go," Mr. Benes said. "I want to talk to you about something."

Lucas and his dad headed back to the hotel. Halfway across the back parking lot Mr. Benes stopped for a second.

"What's up?"

"Your buddy Travis put together some interesting video clips for us this morning."

"Yeah?"

"We have a New Resistance waiter who works at

the lobby café in the Good Hotel in Buenos Aires," Mr. Benes said. "He has a GoPro mounted on his tray and films everything for us."

"Cool."

"Two days ago," Mr. Benes continued, "Charles Magnus had coffee with Interpol's top diamond expert and he sent the Curukians you just met."

"See!" Lucas said. "There is something in the file."

"That's why it's locked up."

Lucas hung his head.

"The other thing I wanted to tell you," Mr. Benes said, "was that after Magnus's meeting with the Interpol agent, he was filmed escorting a woman who looked a lot like your mother, your birth mother, into a van. Some New Resistance kids in Buenos Aires tailed the vehicle to the airport, where Magnus and the lady presumably boarded a plane."

Lucas's eyebrows rose. "That's exactly where Ms. Günerro told me my mother was. In Buenos Aires."

"It's got to be a trap, Lucas," Mr. Benes said. "I sent the pictures to Madame Beach, but apparently she has been in 'an accident.'"

"What?"

"Someone pushed her down the stairs at the Shakespeare and Company bookshop," Mr. Benes said. "She's in intensive care at the hospital in Paris."

"Is she going to be all right?"

"We don't know."

"Hey, Dad?"

"Yes."

"Do you think maybe there's a chance that my mother's alive?"

"Do you want an honest answer?"

Normally when someone asked that question they were going to give you an answer you didn't want to hear.

Lucas swallowed. "Yeah."

"I'm sorry, Lucas, but no, I don't think there's any chance," he said. "She would have made contact already if she was alive."

"Unless she thinks I died on the ferryboat that exploded."

"Enough!"

Lucas dropped his head. "So Ms. Günerro lied."

Mr. Benes stopped in the shade of a palm tree. "Lucas," he said. "You were the one to teach us that everything is backward with the Good Company. What makes you think Ms. Siba Günerro is going to all of a sudden start being nice and help you find your mother?"

Lucas had been told that his mother wasn't alive so many times that he believed it. But telling someone something is different from having proof.

Lucas and his father continued walking between thick green bushes and pink bougainvillea. They rounded the corner and came to the main entrance to the Globe Hotel Las Vegas.

Lining the huge circular drive in front of the hotel

were rows of the finest cars. There were several Aston Martins, a couple of Bugatti Veyrons, and Ferraris and Lamborghinis, too.

"Pretty nice," Mr. Benes said.

"Those are cool," Lucas said, "but they're old-school."

"What do you like?"

"I like that Tesla Model S P85D better."

"Why is that?"

"It doesn't follow everyone else's rules."

Mr. Benes nodded.

Lucas asked, "Why are there so many nice cars here today?"

"It's a car show of some kind," he said. "It's silly, if you ask me, but it's good for business, so we're happy they're staying in our hotel."

"Whose car is this?"

"Why? You want to drive it?"

"Are you kidding?"

There was a rush of wind as the hotel's high-speed roller coaster raced overhead. Lucas and his father watched. The cars hugged the track and banked a hard left, then disappeared into the side of the hotel.

The valet came trotting over with a tablet at his side. "Yes, sir, Mr. Benes?"

"Who's putting this new-car show on?"

"I think it's for a new racing video game that's coming out."

Mr. Benes asked, "Who does the Model S belong to?"

CHAPTER SIX

"The insane car?" said the valet, scrolling through his tablet. "It's registered to . . . to a Mr. Charles Magnus."

THE BIRTH FILE

Mr. Benes's eyes widened. The fact that Charles Magnus had infiltrated the Globe Hotel and the New Resistance unnoticed clearly worried him.

Then he grinned. "Keep your enemies close," he said. "Now get to school while I find out what Magnus is up to."

Lucas pushed through the front revolving doors and into the Globe Hotel Las Vegas.

The main entrance room was a massive atrium with a glass ceiling that sparkled like diamonds. Directly at the back of this room was a ramp leading down into a giant indoor and outdoor swimming pool shaded by palm trees. Guests filled a dining area furnished with plush cobalt-blue booths. Workers in the French bakery were pulling fresh croissants out of the oven, and the smell was driving Lucas crazy.

He walked farther down a mall and passed the Crime Travelers game, where kids try to crack unsolved crimes from all over the world.

At the next corner he caught a glimpse of himself in one of the mirrored columns. His olive skin reminded him of his Argentinean heritage.

CHAPTER SEVEN

Dead or alive—he had to know the truth about his mother.

One place held the answers—the birth chart in the file room. There Lucas could figure out everything. His mother. His father. The Good Company bank accounts. Everything. But he couldn't do it alone.

Fortunately for Lucas, he spotted help coming out of the roller coaster's exit. Paulo Cabral, AKA Jackknife, came sprinting around the corner. The Brazilian's dark hair was now pushed straight up in the front, presumably from the wind on the ride. He was wearing khaki shorts, a T-shirt with an image of Pelé, and a pair of flip-flops.

Just behind him, wearing a long red gown, their friend and fashion queen Nalini Prasad pushed Gini in a stroller. Gini sat quietly doodling with markers on a paper pad.

Jackknife bounded up to Lucas. "I think I know what I want to be when I grow up?"

"What's that?"

"A professional roller coaster rider."

"That's ambitious."

"Jackknife," Nalini said, catching up with them. "I don't think there is such a job."

"I'm so not ready for school to start back," Jackknife said.

"Nobody is," Lucas said.

"Schools have been cutting summertime for years," Jackknife said. "The only reason the break exists in the first place was for the agrarian calendar—so kids could work on the farm."

Lucas said, "It's one of the great wrongs of the world. It's time to turn the schedule upside down. Summer should last nine months, and school should take up only three months of the year."

"Now you're talking," said Jackknife.

"Great," Nalini said sarcastically. "We'd be a third less educated!"

Gini stuck out her tongue and sputtered, "Ppppp."

Before Lucas, Jackknife, Nalini, and Gini could get into any real trouble, they heard Coach Creed's boots clomping across the tile floors.

"I'm madder than a wet rooster," he barked. He gestured toward a back hallway. "Let's get to school now, people."

Pushing the stroller, Nalini led the way.

Jackknife, Lucas, and Coach Creed trailed Nalini to the New Resistance section of the hotel.

At the double doors, Coach typed in a code.

"Lucas, I know what you're thinking," Coach said, hiking up his pants. "You and Jackknife here are planning to break into the file room and get another look at your birth chart."

Lucas gulped. *How is it that grown-ups always know what you're thinking about doing?*

Coach Creed opened the door and held it for the kids. "We can't have any funny business today," he said. "There are probably a lot of kids who have hidden messages in their birth files and baby books. But Charles Magnus is somewhere on the property. And, if one of those charts gets into Good Company hands, it could put us all in danger. That's why no one is getting in there. Is that clear?"

"Yes, sir," they said at the same time.

"Now get to class."

Jackknife and Lucas followed Nalini and the stroller to the end of the hallway, where they got on the elevator.

A moment later the elevator doors opened at the basement level. Nalini pushed Gini into the grand hall. Jackknife and Lucas followed. They had timed it perfectly. The all-school meeting was about to take place. Mr. Siloti was playing Beethoven on the piano, and the smell of doughnuts foretold of an awesome midmorning break in the Grotto café.

With its high-speed moving sidewalks cutting straight down the middle, the cavern looked like a giant version of an ultramodern airport. Sunlight coming from metal tubes in the ceiling lit the cave, making the place look like midday. Opposite the bank of elevators there was the terminal for the train that could take them to the airplane hangar, twenty miles out in the desert.

Students began flooding the hallway. They spilled out of the classrooms and clumped in front of the bank of elevators.

Whoops and hollers greeted Lucas as soon as he

stepped into the hall. He heard his name called out at least ten times. Jackknife and Nalini and Gini moved to the sides, and a semicircle of students formed around Lucas.

"Lucas!"

"All right, Lucas!"

"He's here."

There were new students everywhere, people Lucas didn't recognize, and they seemed to want to get a look at him. Like a monkey in a zoo. Someone stopped the moving sidewalks, and several kids climbed on the handrails trying to get a better view.

"Hey, look over there!"

"The guy in the middle with the messed-up hair right in front of the elevator."

A group of new students knotted together in front of the sidewalk, staring directly at Lucas. Others walked around the group and rubbernecked to catch a glimpse.

Lucas scanned the crowd, looking for familiar faces. He spotted Ms. Dodge the science teacher and Dr. Sherman the English teacher, wearing his signature bowler hat.

Travis was longboarding down the side hallway with a goofy grin on his face.

Kerala was coming out of the girls' bathroom. It looked like she had just caked on even more black Goth makeup. Lucas wondered why she was so weird.

Lily Hill, the girl with red pigtails, was skipping

down the right side. Sora Kowa was sitting on a bench reading a book in Japanese.

With a newspaper under her arm, Astrid stood across from Lucas. If looks could speak, then Lucas knew Astrid was saying to him, "You do not deserve the attention you're getting."

Terry Hines, the short kid with sandy hair who always seemed to get in trouble, emerged from the middle of this crowd.

"Yeah, I was on that bus," Terry said. "It's not true what the French papers are saying about Lucas. He was fighting Günerro for the steering wheel. He didn't wreck her bus on purpose. She did. Lucas saved us all."

Astrid unfolded the *Good Company Gazette* in front of her. Lucas approached and read the headline: GOOD COMPANY SEEKS DAMAGES IN PARISIAN BUS CRASH.

Lucas fell into a fog as self-doubt filled his mind. He argued with himself. *Did I save those kids? Or did I almost kill them?*

Another new student appeared. Lucas recognized him from the back parking lot. He was a massive kid with plenty of facial hair. The boy was wrapped in a thick white serape. Lucas thought he looked like a hairy burrito.

The kid bellowed, "Way to go, Lucas!"

Astrid slid over and stood next to Lucas. "That's Mac," she said.

Jackknife leaned in and added, "As in Big Mac."

"How old is he?" Nalini asked.

"Old," Gini said.

"I think," said Jackknife, "that he's like forty-seven years old."

"He's got a full beard," Lucas said, "like he needs to shave!"

Mac marched toward the crowd that had gathered in front of the elevators.

"He just turned fourteen," Astrid whispered. "And he's going to be your new roommate, Jackknife. I've seen the list."

"Oh no," Jackknife said.

"Wait till you see who *your* roommate is, Lucas," Astrid said.

"Who?"

"Just wait."

ROOMIES

At that moment everyone turned toward the middle of the grand hall. Coming down the center of the long rock corridor was the head of school.

Dr. Joan Kloppers was walking on the now-stalled moving sidewalk, clapping her minuscule hands. Lucas was medium height, but he was at least a head taller than the new head of school.

Dr. Kloppers was the perfect leader for a New Resistance Hotel-School. She wore tiny red glasses on a round happy face that made the little kids at school want to climb in her lap for reading time. She supposedly could read in fifteen different languages.

This morning her long silver jacket drifted behind her as she parted the swarm of new kids who had gathered in front of Lucas. Behind her, a giant ball of yellow fur followed.

Cloudy was a white-faced golden retriever with sweet eyes. The old dog weaved through the mob of students, his tail wagging. Strapped to his back he carried two baskets filled with class schedules. As he passed, kids petted him and picked out their school programs.

Dr. Kloppers climbed a circular staircase that rose about halfway up a stone wall. She stopped at the landing and spoke to the students. The new kids clustered together under the podium.

"Welcome," she said. "Welcome to a new year at the New Resistance Hotel-School in Las Vegas, Nevada!"

The students clapped politely.

Dr. Kloppers was originally South African, and she spoke English with an Afrikaner accent. Beautiful yet forceful.

"As you may know," Dr. Kloppers continued, "this is a school to train students to be world leaders, and while we permit creative rule breaking in the pursuit of some greater good in the future, I must caution you that today there are forces we currently have to deal with that could put several of you in danger."

She gestured toward Jackknife. "Mr. Cabral here, as you may have heard, was nearly brainwashed in Paris by Ms. Siba Günerro, the head of the Good Company. We could have lost this young man." Dr. Kloppers paused for effect. "This is my first year here at this school, but I have been with Mr. Benes and the New Resistance School for nearly two decades, and in that time I've never lost a student, and I don't intend it to happen on my watch." She glared at Lucas. "So I don't need frivolous risk taking or rooftop campouts. Is that clear?"

More head nodding and silence followed this speech.

"I know you are all anxious about getting your room assignments," she said.

The whole cavern erupted in applause with whistles and foot stomping. In a moment the group fell silent, except for Big Mac, who was still clapping louder and *longer* than anyone.

The head of school tapped the screen on the podium.

Lucas could feel his heart beating faster as he worried about his new roommate situation. He had already lost Astrid as a roommate earlier in the summer and was just beginning to come back to the idea of sleeping inside his hotel room again. Alone.

He scooted closer to Jackknife. "I didn't tell anybody who I wanted—did you?"

"Nope," said Jackknife. "Do you really think Astrid was right?"

"Astrid's always right."

"I hope she was joking about me getting Big Mac," Jackknife said, shaking his head. "A guy that big, you just know that when he's asleep, he farts up a massive storm."

Lucas snorted.

Travis slid between Jackknife and Lucas and looped his arms around both of them. He clucked his head toward a kid in a bow tie. "We don't have a dress code now, do we?"

"I feel bad for that kid," Lucas said. "They should have told him."

"What's the school going to say?" Jackknife asked. "Don't dress like a dork?"

Travis said, "At least not on your first day."

"If Big Mac is my roommate," Jackknife said, looking at Lucas, "then that means you're probably getting the bow-tie guy."

Lucas felt a little cheated. He was just starting to feel comfortable in Tier One. He wished he could have given the school some criteria of what kind of kids he liked to hang out with. Like Jackknife and Travis. He didn't need anybody new. Not right now.

Dr. Kloppers looked down at the new students. "Keeping with our nontraditional way of doing things here at the New Resistance, I'll call your names in random order," she said. "From Australia," she announced, "we're proud to have Elizabeth Zerbe!"

There was a huge round of clapping as a twelve-year-old girl wearing a tennis outfit cut through from the new kids' group. She waved excitedly.

The cheers died down, and Dr. Kloppers spoke again. "Elizabeth," she said, "likes tennis, as you can well see, and goes by the nickname Zibby."

Robbie Stafford, a fifth-year-senior Australian, led the cheers and whistles. He called out, "Zibby Zerbe! From Down Under!"

"Zibby," said Dr. Kloppers. "You will be rooming with Lily Hill."

Lily emerged from the crowd, her red pigtails bouncing. She stood next to Zibby Zerbe while some of the other girls gathered around them.

Terry Hines joked out loud, "Lily Hill and Zibby Zerbe?" he said. "What is this, roommate poetry?" Everyone laughed, until he said creepily, "It's like Lu Bunguu."

Dr. Kloppers continued calling out names, but Lucas stopped listening and turned his attention to Travis. He spoke softly so the head of school wouldn't hear him.

"Are you getting a roommate?" Lucas asked.

"I've already got a roommate," Travis said. "Walter Tillman. The dude from DC. He came last year. Remember?"

"I don't know him," said Lucas.

"Me either," Jackknife said, poking his head into the conversation.

Lucas asked, "Is he even still at school?"

"Yeah," Travis said. "You don't see him because he sleeps all the time. I think he's got a disease or something. He's got this eye-twitching thing too."

"Oh yeah," Jackknife said. "I've seen that guy. In the nurse's office. That's your roommate?"

Lucas missed several more names being called out. He turned his attention back to the new roommates.

Dr. Kloppers continued, "Your new roommate is Melissa Rathbone from London."

Wearing black leather pants and a jacket with studded sleeves, Melissa looked more like a Curukian bodyguard than a teenager. She walked up to her new roommate, who was wearing pink yoga clothes. The girls looked at each other, awkwardly shook hands, and then giggled.

Jackknife slapped Lucas on the arm. "I heard Astrid is getting a roommate."

"That's because," Travis said, "she's going to be a resident assistant on the girls' floor."

Dr. Kloppers read the next names. "From Germany we have Emma Weiss." Everyone clapped. "You will be rooming with Li Ha from China."

Two girls, one with long blond curls and the other with straight black hair, literally jumped in the air and clapped. They hugged each other like they had been best friends forever.

Lucas thought that together they looked like a giant tumbleweed of hair.

Two more names were called that Lucas missed. He could sense himself retreating to his old self, his old, insecure self—the one that worried about being noticed.

He thought, *Why is it that the last guy picked is always the last guy picked?*

As Dr. Kloppers read through the next few names on her list, Lucas eyed his possible roommates. If Astrid was right and Jackknife was getting Big Mac as a roommate, then Lucas might actually be getting the guy with the bow tie.

Lucas cataloged the boy's look. His skin was pale, and his cheeks had two red dots. He wore a paisley bow tie, a pink-and-green-striped button-down shirt, perfectly pressed khakis with pleats, and loafers with a shiny shilling in the penny-holding slot. And he had a briefcase!

Then Lucas heard Dr. Kloppers. "This is a mouthful of a name. But we are lucky, fortunate I should say, to have this young man, this *gentleman*, with us. I am privileged to introduce, from the Falkland Islands, Mr. Alister Thanthalon Laramie Nethington the Fourth."

Lucas was trying to figure out if this name was more than one person or not when he heard Dr. Kloppers speak again.

"Your roommate, Alister, will be Lucas Benes."

A group of new students cheered as Alister scuttled in front of the remaining crowd, the dots on his cheeks glowing. Lucas focused on the bow tie. He thought it looked like a little airplane propeller buzzing right at him. Alister set his briefcase down next to Lucas and extended his hand. He gave Lucas a firm handshake, and Lucas nodded but didn't say anything because behind him he heard Jackknife moaning.

"From Damascus, the capital of Syria!" Dr. Kloppers called out. "Mac MacDonald!"

"That's weird," Travis muttered. "Mac from Syria?"

Big Mac came barreling straight through the crowd, knocking two girls to the side. The giant teenager stood in front of Dr. Kloppers's podium like a soldier reporting for duty. Up close the guy really did look like a grown man. He had an unshaven beard on his cheeks and neck, and underneath the white burrito blanket he wore a pair of blue-jean overalls.

"Mac," Dr. Kloppers said, "your new roommate is Paulo Cabral."

Big Mac clapped by beating his hands together like an orangutan. He sprang up on his feet and pumped his arm as if he had just won a tournament. He approached Jackknife with two open palms.

"Jackknife!" he yelled. "I read your whole bio! You're from Brazil. Cool. I already know how to do some of your tricks. Check this out."

The oversize teenager then proceeded to do a standing back flip right there in front of everyone. Lucas had to admit it was cool, but the timing was odd.

Mac raised both arms and gave Jackknife a high ten, nearly suffocating the Brazilian with his armpits. Mac also wore a necklace with a rock pendant that slapped Jackknife in the nose.

The head of school called out a few more names, but Lucas was focusing on trying to say his roommate's name.

Alister Thanthalon Laramie Nethington the Fourth, Lucas practiced in his mind. *The fourth? That means there are three other people with this name?*

Dr. Kloppers's eyes beamed at the kids while she extended her right arm out to welcome them. "We are *all* thrilled to have you with us as part of the New Resistance family. Welcome!"

CHAPTER EIGHT

There came a giddy and clamorous burst of noise and applause with cheering and whistling everywhere.

"A reminder!" Dr. Kloppers said over the ruckus. "Security will be tight tonight and for the foreseeable future. No student may go out of bounds or into restricted areas. That includes the file room, and no sleeping on the roof."

She glared at Lucas.

Lucas nodded obediently, but something told him that he wouldn't be able to follow the rules perfectly.

CODE

Dr. Kloppers clapped again.

"One last thing," she said. "We have a special treat today. The Grotto café will be serving fresh doughnuts. But let's not all rush there immediately."

No one listened. The entire student body of the hotel-school split into two groups, each trying to get to the Grotto fastest. The student lounge and café was located three-quarters of the way down the left-hand side hallway. Half of the students bottlenecked on this side, while the others raced down the right side of the enormous cave and looped back into the café. Either way there would be a wait.

Lucas got in line behind Travis and overheard him talking to a boy with greasy hair.

"That's why I woke you up early," Travis said.

"Yeah," the boy said. "I get bored in English. All those words just make me fall asleep."

"Walter," Travis said. "Everything makes you fall asleep."

Seeing Travis with his roommate reminded Lucas that he might actually make an effort with *his* new roommate. It was always hard to be a new kid in any school. They didn't have to be friends forever, but at least Lucas could be nice to the kid on his first day at school. He turned around and motioned for Alister to catch up with him.

"Thanks," Alister said, trotting up.

The line to get free doughnuts in the Grotto came to a standstill.

Lucas made light conversation. "So you're from the Falklands?" he asked.

"Sure am," Alister said with a Scottish accent. "Born in Scotland, raised in the Falklands."

"Cool."

Alister lowered his eyes and his voice. "I need to talk to you."

"About what?"

He whispered, "FLK in your birth chart doesn't mean Funny Looking Kid."

"What do you mean?"

"It's part of a code."

DOUGHNUTS

Lucas had two burning questions.

What did Alister mean about FLK being a code? FLK—Funny Looking Kid—was simply a signal doctors wrote on birth charts to let people know that the baby had been born odd-looking.

And the real question was how did Alister Thanthalon Laramie Nethington *the fourth* know that doctors had written FLK in Lucas's birth chart in the first place?

By the time Lucas and Alister got to the café entrance, several students were already cutting back through the tide with armloads of doughnuts. The air was thick with sugar.

The Grotto was a classic coffee shop that looked like a library inside a rock cave. The back wall was stone, polished to show the geochronology of the rock. The side wall was covered from floor to ceiling with print books packed so tightly that you could hardly pull one out. Squishy, metal barstools surrounded a huge counter that served peppermint hot chocolates, caramel lattes, muffins, and scones.

And today, doughnuts.

Every booth and barstool was taken.

The kitchen was a perfect place to grill someone—for answers.

Lucas told Alister to follow him. The two boys wormed through the crowded café, back behind the bar, into the kitchen through the double doors.

Cooks in white uniforms were frying all kinds of dough. Lucas recognized an older woman wearing a hairnet. She was loading trays of hot, fresh doughnuts onto an aluminum rack. In the back, a guy wearing headphones was doing the dishes.

Lucas stopped Alister in the middle of the kitchen. "How do you know what was written in my birth chart when it has been in the file room for twelve years?"

"My father knew your mother," Alister said.

"Which one?"

"Which one what?" Alister asked.

"Which mother?" Lucas asked, then he explained. "I had two mothers. A birth mother and Astrid's mother, who adopted me for like a day."

"Well, then," said Alister. "My father knew your birth mother. Luz Kapriss."

Lucas walked behind a tall rack of cooking trays to give the woman wearing the hairnet a hug. Then he took a clean tray, and he and Alister made their selections.

It was doughnut heaven. Glazed, maple, cinnamon-sugar, and plain-cake doughnuts. On the next tray the doughnuts were covered with toppings he had never imagined. Oreos, crushed M&M's, Froot Loops, chocolate bars, marshmallows, and Nutella. On the third tray were some international doughnuts—French crullers, Iranian zulubiyas, Indian jalebis, black-sesame-seed doughnuts from China. And Brazilian sonhos that were supposedly so good you would fall asleep if you ate too many of them.

Lucas and Alister each took a tray filled with doughnuts out of the kitchen and back into the Grotto. Jackknife, Travis, and Astrid crammed into the last open booth. Nalini was carrying Gini, and she sat with them. Astrid shoved the dirty dishes toward the back wall as Lucas and Alister slid the trays onto the tabletop.

Everyone dug in.

Since there was no room on the benches, Lucas and Alister stood next to the table. Alister set his briefcase on the floor. Lucas couldn't wait to find out what Alister knew and why.

"How do you know all this stuff about me?" Lucas asked Alister.

"My father is a banker in the Falklands," Alister said. "And he knew your mother. Your birth mother."

Everyone sitting at the booth stopped eating and listened to Alister.

"Twelve years ago your mother contacted my father," Alister said, "about safeguarding a large sum of money." Alister wiped his mouth with a napkin. "But that's not the real problem."

"Well," Astrid said, "what is?"

"The problem is that no one can locate one of the accounts."

Jackknife put down the doughnut he had just picked up. "Isn't the money in your father's bank?"

"There's some cash, yes," Alister said. "But one of the accounts is the largest safety-deposit box ever—it's actually a shipping container that supposedly has more than just money in it."

"Like what?" Alister asked.

"Mostly diamonds, Bunguu's diamonds to be specific. And supposedly a massive collection of illegal ivory."

"How much is it worth?" Jackknife asked.

"Close to a billion dollars. US."

Lucas was confused. "So where is this container?

"It's all over the world."

Nalini set Gini up on the table. "You're not making a drop of sense, Alister."

Gini began eating doughnuts with both hands. Alister pointed at Gini.

"Case in point," Alister said. "You all have some sort of baby book or birth chart or file. Right?"

Everyone nodded.

Gini burped, "Right."

"Well," Alister said as he glanced over his shoulder. "Sometimes parents hide messages to their children in the kids' baby books."

Nalini said, "Go on."

"The codes to finding these accounts," Alister said, "are hidden in Lucas's birth file."

Astrid said, "Those two Curukians who are in the infirmary wanted Lucas's chart, didn't they?"

"You heard about that?" Lucas asked.

"Everybody did," said Travis.

Alister moved an empty plate and plopped his briefcase onto the table. The kids craned their necks to see what was inside.

The bottom was covered in financial spreadsheets with thousands of little numbers. There were maps of sailing routes and timetables for airplanes, trains, and ships. On top of these papers were little plastic pouches filled with tiny tools, a small computer, an orange keyboard, a watch-sized screen, and a handful of colorful wires.

Jackknife pointed at one of the pouches. "That's a locksmith's toolkit, isn't it?"

"It is."

Travis pointed at the bright orange keyboard. "Is that a Kano computer?"

"It is," said Alister. "But modified to crack some fairly sophisticated encryption software that can easily hack into . . . well . . . a lot."

Lucas saw the plan in his head.

"Hey, Nalini," Lucas said.

"Yeah?"

"Do you have some of Gini's drawings?"

"I do," she said. "Why?"

"Since Gini doesn't have a birth file," Lucas said, "I wanted to start a file for her, and I thought we should start with her artwork."

"Oh that's a great idea."

"Could you get them together?"

"Yeah sure, but when do you want them?"

"Now?" Lucas said hesitantly. "And could you put it in a file outside my room?"

"Sure, we got it."

"Got it," Gini said, clapping.

Astrid asked, "What do you need Gini's drawings for?"

"I may need a decoy," Lucas said.

"For what?" Astrid asked.

"Alister and I have to pick the lock on the file room and have another look at my birth chart."

"What?" Astrid shook her head. "No way."

Jackknife asked, "Can you get in?"

"Whatever it takes," Lucas said.

Alister shut the lid to his briefcase and snapped the locks. "Trust me," he said. "There's nothing I can't get into."

"To me," Astrid said, "it sounds like the only thing you're getting into . . . is trouble."

A MOTHER IS A MOTHER IS A MOTHER

Siba Günerro looked out the window as her black Suburban with tinted windows sped past the security booth at the Good Production Company in Los Angeles, California. The license plate read SALL GOOD. The CEO of the Good Company had just starred in her own marketing infomercial entitled "Rich Like Me."

Ms. Günerro settled in her seat. "Take the scenic road," she said, talking to her driver.

She pushed a red button on the console, and the privacy window between the front and backseat closed with a swoosh.

The driver's name tag read GOPER BRADUS | NUUK, GREENLAND. Goper clicked on the radio and shook his blond mop of a hairdo. He hit the gas and steered the big car through Century City. Once they were on the open road, he twisted the radio knob and turned up the polka music.

Immediately his front-seat passenger began humming along with the song. Goper glanced at his partner, Ekki Ellwoode Ekki, who was rubbing his belly like a pregnant woman. The big man then added a few choice snaps of his fingers to punctuate the drums in the song. He was way off beat. When Ekki started dancing in his seat, Goper had to force a change.

"Give me a doughnut, Ekki," he said.

Ekki slowly stopped humming. He pushed up his round glasses and opened the box of glazed doughnuts sitting on the seat between them. He shoved a glazed cruller into his mouth and handed a chocolate-covered doughnut over to Goper.

With his left hand on the steering wheel, Goper slipped the doughnut onto his right index finger and then gnawed on the edges of the fried dough like it was an edible ring.

Within an hour, the doughnuts were gone, and the Suburban was speeding across the California desert and heading into the rising sun. For another August day the summer heat burned the surrounding countryside, splattering it with the full spectrum of yellow. Traveling ninety-nine miles—one hundred sixty kilometers—per hour, the Suburban blasted into the day.

They stopped at Love's Travel Stop just east of Palm Desert. Ekki got out and bought a six-pack of chocolate milk and four bags of Twizzlers while Goper gassed the car up. They drove east and then turned due north through the Mojave Desert. The summer morning superheated the air, and a haze hovered over the highway. They drove through a national park, where mile after mile of Joshua trees dominated a landscape filled with ocotillo and jumping cacti.

From the backseat Ms. Günerro looked out the window at the scenery.

"I love cacti," she said.

"Yes," said the woman sitting next her. "They're beautiful."

"It's not about beauty," said Ms. Günerro. "A landscape flooded with cacti would make for a perfect natural prison wall."

"Yes," said the other woman. "Or torture field."

"T," said Ms. Günerro, "you've taken cruelty to a new level."

"Plants are organic," T said, "and I like being natural."

"Traveling gives people such good ideas," Ms. Günerro said. "The only thing better than this would be my namesake, Siberia—a frozen desert, but topped with ice cacti!"

"Good pun," T said, chuckling. "Desert/dessert!"

The sound of the tires on the highway changed to hollow tones as the heat warmed the asphalt. Intermittent rays of sun slapped the window, and Ms. Günerro's reflection flashed in the glass, highlighting her salt-and-pepper hair and her cat-eye glasses.

"The sun is dreadful, isn't it?" Ms. Günerro said.

"I'm constantly putting on sunscreen to protect my beauty."

Ms. Günerro chuckled under her breath. Her subordinate was no beauty.

Far from it. T, or Ms. T, as everyone at the Good Company called her, looked like she had been old ever since she was young. The nickname, T, stood for something.

Some thought the name came from the tea she liked to drink, but most in the Good Company assumed T stood for something Terrible. Some said T stood for Trash. Others said it was Toxic for the shipload of chemicals that she once capsized in the middle of the Pacific Ocean. Still others insisted that T's name stood for Torture, and they had the scars to prove it.

Whatever the letter stood for, it was clear that it was not good. She wore glasses thick as Coke-bottle bottoms, and when she smiled, she showed a mouth of teeth that most resembled a horse.

"Do you think we hold on to so much of our beauty," T said with a grin, "because we never had children of our own?"

"I'm confident of it," Ms. Günerro said. "Children turn beautiful women into old hags."

"Speaking of . . ." T said. "How is the 'mother'?"

"Magnus has her now."

"Hmm," T mused. She spoke rapidly, almost nervously. "I can still remember taking that boy's mother out into the Drake Passage. Oh it was cold that day."

"It was Antarctica," Ms. Günerro said. "And you were in international waters."

"What was her name again?"

"Luz Kapriss," Ms. Günerro said as she closed her eyes. "She was a fool."

"All we wanted was a little information." T said. "I still don't understand how we haven't been able to trace those deposits. It's beyond comprehension for those monies *not* to be in a bank or in a safety-deposit box somewhere."

Ms. Günerro said with her eyes now wide open, "What I don't understand is how a cleaning lady was able to come up with a plan to steal my money."

T asked, "There were precious stones also, no?"

"Diamonds galore!" Ms. Günerro said. "And gold and massive quantities of ivory and who knows what Bunguu put in there."

T horse-smiled, cracking the makeup on her face. She had so many layers on that she looked like she had fallen into a cake, and the icing had stuck to her skin.

"So you think the boy will just join us?"

"No," said Ms. Günerro. "I offered him a job with the Good Company already, in Paris. But he fled."

"So what's the plan now?"

"If he thinks his mother is here . . ." Ms. Günerro said.

"Then he'll follow his mother."

"All boys are mama's boys. They're weak. And they live off hope and not facts."

The Suburban rounded another bend, and the sun suddenly grew brighter in the car.

"But, Siba, we've checked every bank in the world,"

CHAPTER ELEVEN

T said. "The fortune has to be somewhere."

"The boy will tell us," Ms. Günerro said. "As soon as he sees the mother, he'll melt. As they all do."

"What is the boy's name again?"

"Lucas."

"Won't Lucas know it's not his mother?"

"A mother is a mother is a mother," Ms. Günerro said. "They're all the same. In fact I would bet that a lot of children would love to have another mother anyway. Change things up a bit. You know? Day in and day out. The same breakfast. The same rules and lectures. Mothers are despicable. They are living proof that foolish consistency is the hobgoblin of little minds."

T took out her compact cosmetic mirror and caked on another layer of makeup.

"No," Ms. Günerro said. "The only person still alive who knew what Lucas's mother really looked like is Madame Adrienne Beach at the Shakespeare and Company bookshop in Paris."

"That's why you had me go to Paris last week," T said. "Ha! I failed to report to you that Madame Beach had an accident."

Ms. Günerro turned up the air conditioner. She gazed out the window at the passing sign. It read LAS VEGAS 100 MILES.

THE PLAN

Since the beginning of time, human beings have been protected by a sixth sense. It was the feeling, the knowing, you got when you met someone and they made you feel uncomfortable—it was a feeling some people called the heebie-jeebies.

Lucas's sixth sense was on high alert, but he didn't know why.

During lunch Lucas followed Alister back to their hotel room to unpack Alister's bags.

They hadn't been in the room but a few minutes when Nalini and Gini knocked at the door.

"Here's the file you wanted," Nalini said.

Lucas took the folder and opened it.

Inside there were hundreds of pages of Gini's colorful drawings, scribbles, doodles, diagrams, and even some pages that looked like cryptic doctor notes. Some were written in crayon, others in pen and pencil.

"Perfect," Lucas said, putting the folder on the bed. He motioned for the others to follow him out.

Cloudy was sleeping next to a cleaning cart just outside Travis's room. As Alister passed by the cart, he snatched a blank key card from the bottom shelf.

When the stairwell door screeched open, Cloudy growled, a hint of distrust in his eyes.

Wrapped in a white Mexican serape, Mac MacDonald lumbered down the hall. The big kid was eating a doughnut and smelled like a swimming pool.

"Pew!" Gini said.

Mac snarled at the baby in the stroller.

"You been for a swim?" Lucas asked.

"I love to swim," Mac said. "I used to go down to the Dead Sea in Jordan and race."

"That's cool," Lucas said.

"The water there is really salty," Nalini said.

"I heard," Alister added, "that people read books while floating on their backs in the Dead Sea. Is that true?"

"Not everyone floats," he said.

That uncomfortable feeling—the heebie-jeebies— crept up Lucas's spine and settled into his shoulders. Something was just not right with this kid supposedly from Syria.

Cloudy circled behind Mac, sniffing the doughnut in his hand.

Mac ignored the dog and changed the subject. "So," he said. "I hear you're named after your mother."

"Yeah," Lucas said hesitantly.

"She was a cleaning lady, wasn't she?"

"Yeah," Lucas said, "but that's not in my school bio. How would you know that?"

"I know a lot of things," Mac said.

It was definitely time for this conversation to end.

Suddenly Cloudy leaped at the half-eaten dough-nut. As Mac swatted him away, he fell backward and onto the floor. His serape flapped open in the front, exposing his cowboy boots, a Speedo swimming suit decorated with the Syrian flag, and a black stone necklace.

Nalini shrieked at the sight, and Gini broke out in laugher. Mac MacDonald quickly covered himself and stood back up.

"Not funny, Benes," he said, and took off down the hall.

As soon as Mac was gone, Travis cracked his door open. "Did Mac just ask you about your mother?"

"Yeah, and I have no idea how he knew that," said Lucas.

"He gives me the creeps," said Nalini.

"More than that," Travis said. "I was hacking into some old databases this morning, and the informa-tion in Mac's school application doesn't match with his past. It's like he has no history."

"That's like Kerala," Lucas said. "She just showed up one day at the Globe Hotel Luxembourg."

Nalini asked, "How would he know about Lucas's mother?"

"I don't have an answer for that," Travis said.

Lucas asked, "Did you tell my dad about the misinformation in Mac's application?"

"I did," said Travis. "He said if Mac was going to be a problem, then we should keep our friends close and our enemies closer."

"What's that supposed to mean?" Nalini asked.

"It means," Travis explained, "that if you keep your enemies close, you can keep an eye on them."

"It also could mean," Alister said, "that Mac and the Curukians that Lucas met in the parking lot are here for the same reason."

"To steal Lucas's birth file?" Travis said.

"Yes." Alister picked up his briefcase. "Which is why Lucas and I are going to get it before they can."

Lucas and Alister fled down the stairs, skipping two and three steps at a time. They passed the infirmary where Tall Boy and Muscle Shirt were being taken care of. Lucas took a shortcut through the laundry area and stopped at the file room door.

Alister inspected the locks. He set the briefcase on the floor, opened it, and pulled out his tools.

"Boot up that Kano computer," he said. "And hook up the wires, would you please? This first lock will take a second longer than I thought."

"Why?"

"This is a seven-cylinder pin-and-tumbler lock," Alister said. "Normally there are only five."

While Lucas got the computer ready, Alister picked the lock. He inserted a small wrench into the bottom of the dead bolt and began raking the cylinders.

The lock clicked open.

"Amazing," Lucas said.

"Now for the electronic lock," he said.

Alister inserted a wire into the DC power socket on the base of the lock.

"This is used to program the lock with the hotel's site code, but it also gives us access to the thirty-two-bit key from the lock's memory."

He inserted the blank key card into the door handle slot, and then typed on the keyboard. "Now we just send the same code back to the lock itself, and . . ."

Click.

The door to the file room unlocked.

"How do you know this stuff?"

"I want to work in international banking, and if you're going to know something, you need to know all sides. How people make money and how people steal money. And every two-bit thief knows how to pick a lock. That's why I'm a hacker and a member of The Open Organisation of Lockpicks. They call us TOOOLs."

"You said it, not me!"

"Ha-ha."

Alister loaded the stuff back into the briefcase and took out a flashlight. Lucas opened the door, and they stepped into the dark room.

MILES OF FILES

The file room was so quiet that Lucas could hear his heart beating. He knew he was breaking the rules, but he had to keep information away from the Curukians. He calmed his breath and closed the door gently so the blinds wouldn't clack against the glass.

Alister scanned the room with the flashlight.

There was a sitting area that looked like a doctor's office with chairs and tables and magazines. Behind a counter there were rows and rows of files.

They tiptoed into the back, and Alister shone the flashlight on the tops of the cabinets. The first one read A–B. The other side read C–E.

"Benes or Kapriss?"

"Benes," Lucas said with a shrug. "But they may have moved it."

"You don't even know who you are, do you?"

"I'm working on it."

They slipped between the two giant cabinets, passed the *A*s, and stopped at the *B*s. Crammed in side by side were thousands of file folders with different colored tags on the ends.

Some of the files were big fat books, like baby books

jammed with pictures of grandma and first birthday parties. Some were so thin that they had to pull them out just to read the names.

Alister mumbled the names as he pulled out the folders. "Baak, Babbit, Babineaux . . ." he whispered. "Who are these people?"

Lucas said, "Kids who live in other Globe Hotels, I guess."

"Benes!" Alister said. He pulled out the one Benes file. It read ASTRID. "Let's try Kapriss."

The file they were looking for was so fat that it nearly jumped off the shelf. It was light blue with an *x* marked on the side. It read, KAPRISS, LUCAS (BENES).

It wasn't a simple birth chart, but rather a group of file folders, each bulging with papers of all kinds wrapped with rubber bands. The first chart number was 330816-1.

The number meant something to Lucas, but at the moment he couldn't put his finger on it.

Alister set the folders on the floor and spread out the loose papers.

There were notes written in different languages—Chinese, Dutch, Italian. Some of the papers had browned. A few pages felt like they would crumble into bits. Some were handwritten, and some had been typed and had splotches of Wite-Out painted over mistakes. There were drawings of spirals and Greek letters.

Alister snatched up a note card that was embossed

with the letters ATLNIII. "These are my dad's initials."

The card was addressed to Luz Kapriss, The Good Hotel, Buenos Aires. Alister studied the card. "I can't read this."

Lucas took the note and flipped it open. "It's written in Esperanto."

He read:

Mia Luz,
Kiam mia filo, Ivy, estas malnova sufiĉa, mi sendos lin en serĉo de ĉi tiu dosiero desentrañar via mistero.
Triple Sticks

Lucas worked out the translation.

"My Luz. When my son, Ivy, is old enough, I will send him in search of this file to unravel your mystery. Triple Sticks"

"Not Ivy," Alister said, his eyes wide open. "I. V. That's what my dad used to call me."

"Why?"

"My name is Alister Thanthalon Laramie Nethington the Fourth. 'The fourth' written in Roman numerals is IV—Ivy." He glanced at the front of the card and pointed at the ATLNIII. "That's my father. Alister Thanthalon Laramie Nethington the Third— Triple Sticks."

Lucas shook his head. "He should have saved everybody a lot of trouble and just called you something easy, like Al."

Having Alister around gave Lucas new eyes for this old chart.

While Lucas flipped through the cards that were clasped to the file, Alister stacked the pieces of paper.

The first couple of pages Lucas had recently seen when they were looking for this mysterious code. It showed his name and the Good Hospital in Tierra del Fuego. He saw the notes about his birth and messages that said Lucas's head was "rather large" and that he had "a congenital case of cowlicks."

Bed-head since birth, Lucas thought.

He spotted the note where the doctors had listed him as an FLK—Funny Looking Kid. But this time he noticed a series of numbers next to the letters *FLK*.

He looked at Alister. "You said you knew what FLK meant," he said, and he spun the paper toward Alister.

"FLK means Funny Looking Kid," Alister said, "but it is also the ISO country code for the Falklands."

"So how does this fit into my birth chart?"

"Apparently your mother was some sort of math genius."

"She was a cleaning lady."

"That's partly true," Alister said as he took over the file and began flipping through the papers. "But my father worked in international banking his whole life and knew your mother. He said that she was one of the smartest people he'd ever met."

Lucas said, "It doesn't make sense."

"It does if you understand higher-level math," Alister said.

"Yeah," said Lucas.

"Did you ever wonder why you're taking university-level math and you're only fourteen?" Alister asked. "It's called genes. And not the ones you wear."

Lucas had thought about his olive-colored skin and his bed-head hair before, but had never really thought about why he was the way he was, why he was able to memorize city maps, and why calculus was easy for him.

Both boys stared at the pages. Alister flipped one after another while Lucas tried to make sense of them.

"According to my dad," Alister said, "there are supposedly three types of numbers. There's one for a shipping container, another number or code for the destination or place, and the third number for time on the calendar."

Lucas stopped cold. He could sense movement on the other side of the door. He killed the flashlight and parted a clump of files to peer through to the door. Outside in the hallway someone was jiggling keys.

"Shut up you idiot," one voice said.

Alister's eyes bugged out, and he mouthed, "Who is it?"

Lucas shrugged. Alister dumped Lucas's main file into the briefcase.

Before Alister had time to spin the locks on the briefcase, two figures entered the dark office.

Lucas crept behind the filing cabinets, and Alister clutched the unlocked briefcase under his arm.

Flashlight beams flickered through the file folders.

"Let's get what we need," said one of the voices, "and get out of here."

"Don't worry," said the other. "That Texan coach won't wake up until we're long gone."

Lucas noted the Eastern European accents. He knew these guys. Muscle Shirt and Tall Boy had obviously done something to Coach Creed and broken out of the infirmary.

Tall Boy chuckled. "That was a good idea to fake being hurt in the parking lot this morning to get us in here."

"It was easier than I planned," Muscle Shirt said. "I thought that Lucas kid was supposed to be some superstar."

"What was that he was trying to do? Tae kwon do?"

"More like tae kwon don't."

A knot formed in Lucas's gut.

The birth files in that room were sacred to everyone at the New Resistance. They were the keys to the kids' identities, and losing them would erase their histories.

Lucas had gone easy on those guys, and now he was paying for it. Once burned, twice shy.

He would have to up his game.

Lucas and Alister eased around the end of the giant cabinet marked J–L. Muscle Shirt passed just on the other side of F–H.

A light hit Alister's briefcase.

"What's that?" Muscle Shirt said.

"What's what?"

"There's somebody in here."

"I got this," Lucas said, whispering. He snatched the briefcase from Alister. "Take off your bow tie."

Tall Boy moved closer.

"My tie?" Alister asked.

"Just unknot it!"

Alister undid his tie, and Lucas moved into the aisle. Muscle Shirt aimed the flashlight at him.

Lucas started to swing the briefcase toward Tall Boy's head, but he remembered that the case was still unlocked. Tall Boy threw a flurry of solid fists. Lucas sidestepped them, and the files behind him took the force of the blows. Papers flew everywhere.

Lucas ducked and locked the briefcase.

Tall Boy stumbled and nearly fell from the missed hits.

Lucas rose and crashed the briefcase up into Tall Boy's chin. Then he smashed the side of the case across the boy's face. Tall Boy buckled over, groaning.

"I hope you approve of my skills now," Lucas said.

Then Lucas smacked the briefcase on the back of the boy's head. Tall Boy dropped to the floor. Holding his face, he curled into a ball.

Out of the corner of his eye, Lucas spotted Muscle Shirt accelerating down the aisle toward him. Lucas swung the briefcase, jabbing its corner into the boy's gut.

When the case skittered to the floor, Muscle Shirt leaned down to pick it up.

Lucas said, "I'm not going to let you take the one thing that my mother left me."

Lucas spun and slipped the bow tie from Alister's collar. He looped it over Muscle Shirt's head and around his neck. The boy dropped the briefcase, clawing the tie away from his neck.

"What are you doing?" Muscle Shirt complained.

"You didn't like my tae kwon do this morning?" Lucas asked. "Well maybe you'll like my *bow tie* kwon do."

"Stop!" the boy screamed.

Still holding Muscle Shirt from behind, Lucas said, "Don't worry. I'm not really going to hurt you." He caught his breath. "But Alister is."

When Alister stepped forward, guarding his face with his fists, Lucas quickly realized the mistake. Alister wasn't trained to fight at all.

Muscle Shirt arched his back and used Lucas's chest as a fulcrum.

As Alister moved closer, he cocked his right arm.

Muscle Shirt's feet rose, his knees bent. Then he kicked Alister square in the chest. The force sent Alister careening against the back wall.

CHAPTER THIRTEEN

Muscle Shirt squirmed out of the bow tie and spun around to face Lucas, ready to fight. The boy reached in his pocket, pulled out a scalpel, and tossed the safety cap to the floor.

"You stole that from the school's infirmary!"

"So what?" Muscle Shirt said, glancing at the knife in his hand.

A tiny but perfect distraction.

Lucas took advantage of the moment and lunged at the boy, shoving him against the metal cabinet. The scalpel clattered on the floor.

"My back," the boy said as he slid to the ground.

"Take an ibuprofen," Lucas said, "and call me in the morning."

Somewhere outside the file room, Lucas could hear more commotion. He knew security would be on its way. And they would find these boys and the mess they'd made and Coach Creed, too.

Lucas slowed his breathing to reduce the adrenaline rush. Alister snatched up his bow tie and briefcase while Lucas helped him up. The two boys slipped into the hallway and headed upstairs to their hotel room to figure out what the codes in the birth chart really meant.

THE HOTEL BILL

Holding the beat-up briefcase, Alister opened the door to their hotel room.

On the carpet there was an envelope.

A bill? Lucas thought. *We're students. We don't get hotel bills.*

Alister removed the key card and held the door half open with his foot. Lucas picked up the envelope and lifted the flap. The folds in the paper were not even. Someone had hurried. He slid his finger along the creases to make the paper flatter.

Eleven words were centered on the otherwise blank sheet of paper.

If you want to see your mother, look out the window.

MESSAGE IN A CAR

Doing the same thing as everyone else, following the herd, never really felt right to Lucas.

He raced to the window and craned his head down toward the side parking lot where the trash dumpsters were. Parked cockeyed across the white lines was the Tesla Model S. To block the glare, Lucas put his hand to his brow. There were two people in the car. In the passenger seat there was a woman with long black hair.

My mother? Lucas thought.

It wasn't logical, and he knew it. But that tiny bit of hope that had been asleep in his heart for twelve years awakened. Lucas stared. His insides were being pulled by a tug-of-war between reason and hope.

Long black hair.

She looked like the woman in the picture he had seen at the Shakespeare and Company bookshop. But that picture had been taken before he was born.

There were too many weird coincidences.

The phone rang, echoing in the quiet hotel room.

The sound snapped him out of his trance.

Lucas looked back as if he'd never heard such a sound.

Alister tossed his briefcase onto the bedspread and ran to the nightstand.

"Answer it," Lucas said.

"Hello?"

Then he held the phone out for Lucas. "It's for you."

Lucas grabbed it and put the receiver to his ear. "Hello?"

A man's voice said three words. "Bring the file."

The line went dead and Lucas hung up.

"They want the file," Lucas said.

"What are you going to do?"

Long black hair. It could be her.

Lucas knew if he did nothing then he would always wonder.

Out the window, Alister kept watch on the back parking lot.

Lucas sat on the bedspread and opened Alister's briefcase. He looked at his file and at the number written on the tab. He finally recognized it as the number *phi*, backward: 330816-1.

He borrowed a pen from the briefcase and put Gini's folder in his lap. On the tab he wrote the number *pi*, also backward: 295141-3.

Then Lucas put the folder under his shirt and left the room and went downstairs. He cracked the door open and looked out. In his mind he set the plan. He would run out to the car and look at the woman. He knew he would know instantly.

The Tesla turned one hundred eighty degrees to

face the driver toward the hotel. Lucas knew this would be trouble because behind the wheel was Charles Magnus.

Lucas clutched the folder in his arms and pushed the door open with his butt. He jogged diagonally across the parking lot through the heat and toward the Tesla.

The trunk located on the front of the Tesla clicked open. Then the driver's-side door opened.

Lucas glanced through the interior and zeroed in on the woman's profile. She had long black hair like his mother. She had beautiful olive-colored skin.

Argentinean?

Wearing a white security-guard shirt with a walkie-talkie clipped to the shoulder, Magnus stepped out and pushed Lucas to the front of the Tesla.

"Get in," he said, pointing to the small luggage area.

"In the front trunk?"

"Yeah," Magnus said. "In the frunk."

Magnus glanced over his shoulder. With his forearm he knocked Lucas into the compartment.

Lucas folded himself into the tiny space between the front bumper and the driving compartment. He was still trying to position his legs and the rest of his body when Magnus closed the lid and plunged him into darkness.

CHAPTER 16

ARE YOU MY MOTHER?

For Lucas, the claustrophobia settled in.

Crammed in the tiny space, he understood what a coffin must surely feel like. He patted the walls around him. They seemed to be squeezing him and sucking the air from his lungs. His heart raced as he pounded on the car's hood, which was just above his head. There was no exit.

The engine whispered as the Tesla eased around the back parking lot. The car hit a speed bump in the parking lot. Lucas knew he couldn't worry about the boneheaded moves he'd already made. You can never fix the past. And he would surely make more mistakes in the future. All he could do was focus on now.

This is worse than kidnapping, he thought. *I did this to myself. No one knows where I am. And I have no idea where I am being taken or how I'm getting out of this.*

Lucas gulped in a giant breath of stale air, and his whole body calmed down. Without sight he navigated by sound. He could hear other cars.

As the tires rolled over the curb and into the street, Magnus spun the car to the right. Lucas tried to visualize where he was. He could sense the map in his head. He guessed they were passing a box store and the 7-Eleven he and Jackknife liked to walk to.

In the dark trunk his mind drifted back to why he had done what he had done. Lucas knew that he had to know for sure about his mother. He had to know if it was possible for her to be alive after this many years.

Magnus took the next turn without slowing down. He cut a sharp left, and the centripetal force tossed Lucas to the right, rocking him against the walls. Lucas heard the monorail buzzing overheard, and then the Tesla stopped.

Magnus hit the INSANE button, and in a matter of seconds the Model S P85D rocketed to sixty miles—nearly one hundred kilometers—per hour.

The force pinned Lucas to the back of the frunk. As they weaved in and out of traffic, Lucas tried to trace every twist and turn.

A few minutes later the Tesla slowed. They bumped up a curb, and Lucas heard a garage door rumble open. Magnus spun the car and put it in reverse. The sound of the scrolling door grew fainter.

A second later the acoustics changed to the interior of a building of some kind. Then silence. The two car doors opened.

Magnus opened the frunk and motioned for Lucas to move. He crawled out clutching the birth chart. Magnus hit a button, and the huge roller door began to descend like a big set of teeth locking them inside a giant mouth.

Before the light went out, Lucas took a photograph of everything with his mind.

He presumed they were in the back of a hotel, which he figured was the Good Hotel Las Vegas. The space was some sort of private entrance and could hold only two cars.

The other spot was taken by a black Suburban with tinted windows. The license plate read SALL GOOD.

The giant roller door came to a close, and the garage fell into darkness, lit only by a bulb above a metal door that led doubtlessly inside.

Magnus held out his hand for the woman with long black hair. He then pointed Lucas and the woman up a flight of concrete steps to the metal door. Lucas glanced at the woman in the low light.

The head of Good Company Security led them down a long corridor that smelled of onions.

The walkie-talkie speaker on his shoulder screeched. "Magnus?"

He pushed a button and spoke. "Yes."

"We've got a problem with our audio and video security," Ms. Günerro said. "Get in here, now."

"What about the boy and his mother?" Magnus asked.

"Put them in the holding room for a minute. It'll give them some mother-son time that I'm sure they need."

CHAPTER SIXTEEN

At the end of the corridor Magnus opened a door to a walk-in refrigerator. A single bulb hanging from the center of the room cast a cone of light on the concrete floor. On the left, soda cans filled the shelves. At the back, there were step stools. On the right was a corrugated tin wall.

"Ms. Günerro will be with you shortly," Magnus said. "Help yourself to the drinks."

He left the room, and the refrigerator door closed behind him.

Lucas and the woman with long black hair sat on two stools and faced each other. Lucas dropped the birth file on the floor near his feet. Then he opened a Coke, took a sip, and set the can down.

A lifetime of questions burned inside of Lucas's gut. Doubt and hope vied for the same spot in his heart. His eyes adjusted to the low light as he got straight to the point.

"Are you my mother?"

As she gathered her words, the woman with long black hair stared at Lucas. In the low light Lucas could finally see her eyes.

Instinctively he knew.

And he had a foolproof method for bringing out the truth.

WHEN YOU KNOW, YOU KNOW

It was like this.

If you lived in a hotel with kids who were from all over the world and who had no real history, no parents, no personal story about where they grew up, no favorite swimming spot, no grandma's house, no sports club or park, then you were sure to meet a lot of kids who were in a constant state of lying. Fabricating the truth. Inventing a past.

Like anyone, Lucas wanted to know who he was. But without his own history to rely on, he had himself been guilty of lying about his childhood. He desperately wanted to know his past. Since there wasn't one, he'd had to create one.

Lucas had been untruthful to himself forever—certainly about his birth mother. He knew she couldn't be alive. He had done the math a million times. She would have contacted him before this. She knew the nuns in Tierra del Fuego, where she had dropped Lucas off with the birth chart. The nuns knew John Benes. It would have been a simple phone call. She could have sent a message. She could have used Morse code.

Somehow. Some way.

Sitting in this refrigerator all alone with this woman, Lucas came to a new and scary idea. The woman in front of him might be a spy.

For Ms. Günerro.

Lucas had three favorite ways to suss out a liar.

Number one: The best liars are creative. Think Siba Günerro. *Tell a lie so big they have to believe it.* Creative liars used the right side of the brain, so their eyes tended to veer left when they were making up a story.

Second on Lucas's list was the fake smile. It was a sign of deep, uncomfortable lying. And third, giving too much unimportant information was the classic badge of a novice.

This woman did all three at once.

Her first words to Lucas were: "I remember the day I took you to the nuns." Her eyes dropped hard to the left as her right brain began colorizing her obviously memorized story.

Lucas thought, *Mothers always say, "I remember the day you were born."*

The woman picked some lint from her dress. "You had just been born and it was a beautiful sunny day and you were wearing this cute blue-and-red vinyl jumpsuit and it had little white buttons made of ivory on the front. The housekeepers at the Good Hotel Buenos Aires had given me these wonderful baby gifts . . ."

Lucas stopped listening. He was born on the solstice, June 21. In the Southern Hemisphere. The first day of winter.

". . . and I walked you through a fields of fachine flowers and there were . . ."

Lucas thought, *There are no flowers in winter.*

". . . and you were so sweet," she continued.

Okay, he thought, *that probably is true.*

The woman scratched her nose, and Lucas was sure he saw a flash of guilt in her eyes. "I was heartbroken to do what I was doing. I hope you'll forgive me, Lucas, but Ms. Günerro would have killed us both. It was safer for you—and for me, too. I hope you believe me. It was Madame Beach's idea for me to take you to the nuns."

Lucas nodded. Not to agree with what she was saying but to confirm what he already knew. The final and most convincing way to spot a liar was to ask the unexpected. What Alister said came back to Lucas. "Apparently your mother was some sort of math genius."

"Do you know what pi is?"

"Pie?" she asked. "Of course. I love pies. Meat pies—empanadas—are my favorite."

"I mean the number pi," he said. "Three point one four and so on."

"I don't know the number pi."

Lucas couldn't imagine someone not knowing the number pi. He had memorized more than eleven hundred digits for his eleventh birthday.

Lucas kept up the inquisition. "Do you know what phi is?"

"It sounds Greek," she said.

"It is."

"Is it a number or something to eat?"

"It's a number," Lucas said. "One point six one and so on. It's called the golden ratio."

"I'm a cleaning lady," she said. "Why would I know math like that?"

"Because my mother was a math genius," Lucas said. "And you're not my mother, are you?"

The woman with long black hair stammered as she started to defend herself. She gulped, swallowed, and lowered her head.

"I'm very sorry, Lucas," she said. "Ms. Günerro killed my husband, and she and Magnus made me try to trick you. I knew you would know fachine flowers don't grow in winter."

"Did you know my mother?"

"I took her job at the Good Hotel in Buenos Aires," the woman said. "I took the job after Ms. T took your mother out to the Drake Passage. And your mother never returned."

Lucas could feel the lump in his throat growing.

It's one thing to think about someone not being alive. But to feel it. To feel the forever. That hurt. It felt like his sports-induced asthma coming on again. But different this time.

His lip drooped and his esophagus tightened. His lungs shrank and his breath shortened. The lack of oxygen tightened his tear ducts. He could feel it coming. He knew he had been feeling this his whole life.

From the moment his birth mother saved his life by putting him with the nuns in Tierra del Fuego, he had felt the loss. A life without his mother. His whole life. And now he knew for sure. The hope he'd held until now withered and died.

Lucas's body quivered as the reality of being without his mother set in. His shoulders rolled forward. The woman with long black hair opened her arms, and Lucas leaned in and dropped his arms to his sides. He fell into the woman's hug and buried his head and sobbed.

She let Lucas cry for a few minutes, then said, "Lucas, your mother believed in you, and she was very brave to hide you away."

"I should have known," he said. "Ms. Günerro's a liar and does everything backward."

"You can't always believe what people tell you."

"I know," Lucas said. "Even when you want it to be true."

"I'm sorry, Lucas," she said.

"Why didn't anyone arrest Ms. Günerro or Ms. T?"

"There was no real proof. Everyone said that Ms. T and your mother were lost in international waters. But a few days later, Ms. T quietly returned, alone."

Lucas nodded. "That explains it," he said. "International waters begin twelve nautical miles offshore. Anything can happen."

"I don't know the law."

"It doesn't matter," he said. "I'm sure it's pretty hard to get the police to go into the waters around Antarctica, anyway."

"I wish I could bring your mother back, but some people care more about money than they do people. I'm really sorry."

"Me too," he said, and then just as he was about to get mad, Lucas stepped back and folded his arms. "I need to know what she did with the money."

"I'll tell you what I know," she said. "But first I want to tell you a story."

"About what?"

"About who you are."

UNDER YOUR NOSE

The woman with long black hair sighed. She leaned forward and looked Lucas in the eyes.

"There's something you need to know about your family," she said.

"What?"

"Your mother's father—your grandfather," she explained, "used to be a diamond merchant."

Lucas wrinkled an eyebrow. He'd never heard mention of his grandfather.

"Many years ago, he and some friends owned a diamond mine in the Belgian Congo, in the heart of Africa." She paused. "The mine was very profitable, and your grandfather shared with everyone there."

"But . . ."

"But there was a unit in the Congolese army led by General Bunguu, Lu Bunguu's father, who didn't like foreigners. He took over the government in a coup, and in doing so he stripped your grandfather and his friends of everything they owned."

Lucas sat wide-eyed.

"After that, your grandparents and your mother were forced to leave Africa. They moved to Argentina to work for the mines there."

"Silver mines?" Lucas asked.

"Probably—Argentina *does* mean 'land of silver.'"

The woman with long black hair crossed her arms. "But soon after, the Bunguu family hired Dr. Günerro, who was Siba's father, and was this crazy scientist from Antarctica. Together, the Bunguus and the Günerro family teamed up to create the Good Company."

The light in Lucas's mind clicked on. "So the Good Company was started with money that was stolen from my grandfather?"

"Yes."

Lucas didn't know what to say.

"After that, your grandfather died, and your mother had to start working when she was eleven. When she was a teenager, Madame Beach hired her to work at the Good Hotel as a housekeeper. From then on your mother kept a journal on everything the Good Company did illegally."

Lucas didn't blink.

"And then, one day this container showed up at the Good Hotel in Buenos Aires. Inside were files, old photographs of your grandfather when he owned the mine, cash, *and* diamonds—Kapriss diamonds from the mine in Africa. Plus some ivory tusks that Lu Bunguu had thrown in as a gift to Ms. Günerro."

"So where's the container now?"

"The story is that your mother knew a man in the Islas Malvinas."

"The Falklands?"

"Yes, but in Argentina we call the islands by a different name," she continued. "This man was an English or Scottish banker, I believe. I think he liked your mother, so he helped her hide the container by shipping it around the world."

"But where?"

"The container travels to hotels all over the world," the woman said. "When it arrives, the head of housekeeping signs the paperwork and sends it back out to the next hotel."

"Why wouldn't they just steal it?"

"Because when your mother was at the Good Conference in Paris she made a pact with hundreds of housekeepers worldwide. They knew that if Ms. Günerro was caught in business with Bunguu and stolen Kapriss diamonds, she would go to jail."

"So are all housekeepers spies against the Good Company?"

"Most of us are," she said.

"Which hotels does the container go to?"

"They're all Good Hotels on the water."

"You mean the money Ms. Günerro has been looking for has been right under her nose in her own company?"

"Yes," she said. "I think your mother liked the irony."

"So how do I find it?"

"The only way to find the container is to decipher

the codes in your birth chart," she said, pointing to the file on the floor.

"But . . ."

She winked. "I know those are not the real documents."

As Lucas picked up the file, the corrugated tin wall behind them rattled and began to groan as it opened.

After a series of mechanical clangs, the wall rose up like a portcullis in a castle's gate into the ceiling, revealing a large, elegant room. Lime-green couches and paintings of pink flowers filled the office.

Six Curukians greeted Lucas and the woman with long black hair. The boys wore khaki shorts and tan shirts and all had thin blond peach-fuzz mustaches. Clear plastic cords spiraled from their ears.

At the back of the room was a flight of stairs with a chrome banister. And next to it, behind an enormous titanium desk, sat none other than Siba Günerro.

THE WRITING IS ON THE DESK

The CEO of the Good Company wore what to Lucas looked like a mermaid dress. An all-white veil studded with diamonds melted into a gown so white and so bright that it made Lucas's eyes wince.

Ms. Günerro clapped her hands three times like a schoolteacher getting the attention of a classroom. At the end of the third clap, two of the older Curukian boys approached Lucas and took the folder from him.

One of the boys set the file on Ms. Günerro's desk. Lucas hoped she wouldn't open it and discover Gini's drawings.

Lucas inched forward. He was now close to Ms. Günerro. The desk legs were made of elephant tusks. Pure ivory. And the surface sparkled. It was inlaid with a mixture of gold and diamonds that swirled across the workspace in an endless spiral. Lucas immediately saw the math behind the design. The golden spiral appeared to form quarter-circles that were slightly angled. Her desktop was a math problem. A logarithm. Lucas committed the design to his map memory.

He needed to make sure she didn't look in the file.

"That's mine!" Lucas yelled as he lunged.

The two other Curukians sprang up and blocked his forward motion.

"When we were in Paris," Ms. Günerro said, "we made a deal on the bus, as I recall."

The woman with long black hair grabbed Lucas's wrist, which felt odd. Lucas started to shake her hand away, but then the woman squeezed his arm.

Sometimes you just have to play along until you know the rules of the game.

"You saved my life, Lucas," Ms. Günerro said. "I could have drowned on that bus. What you did was heroic. For me it was a rebirth, a renaissance, a baptism of sorts. Since I left Paris, my perspective on life has changed. I want everything to be good and right. You and your mother here belong together. All people should have what rightfully belongs to them." She tapped the file folder with her fingernail. "This birth chart rightfully belongs to me because I own the Good Orphanage, and therefore I own all the documents that were created there."

"But it's about me," Lucas argued.

Ms. Günerro shook her head. "I told you that I would trade you this birth chart for your mother," she said. "And I have delivered my part of the deal. And you too have complied with your end of the bargain."

"But . . ."

"Let's drop everything and read," she said strumming her fingers on the folder. "Shall we?"

She handed the file to one of the Curukians, and the boy opened the birth chart.

He bumbled the words. "If you ewe blaaa can dummmba." The boy stopped reading. "It's too blurry."

"Give me that," Ms. Günerro said, taking the file. She slapped it down on the desk. "All you need is this little number on the outside," she said with a grin. "Two nine five one four one dash three. That's the container we're looking for."

Ms. Günerro reached into the top right-hand drawer and snatched a handful of frozen green peas. A thin puff of dry-ice smoke swirled up and into the air.

Part of Lucas wanted to destroy Ms. Günerro for what she had done or what she had let happen to his mother, and his grandfather, too. But this was not the time to quarrel about things he couldn't change. He needed someone to argue for him and with him, like Astrid. But he would have to do it on his own. He channeled his sister.

Lucas asked in the snippiest way possible, "Why do you always have dry ice with you?"

Ms. Günerro was calm. "It reminds me of home."

"Home?" Lucas said. "I can't imagine you having a home."

"When my father was a scientist in Antarctica, my parents kept our home ice cold. They knew I would adapt," Ms. Günerro said. "Besides, my mother was from Siberia, which is why I am called Siba."

Lucas blurted, "You're named for a frozen tundra?"

"Frozen tundra, Freon, dry ice," Ms. Günerro said. "It all keeps me cool so that I make the best decisions."

Lucas pointed at the desk legs. "Decisions like . . . killing two elephants so you could have a dumb desk?"

"Elephants are fat," Ms. Günerro said. "And they take up too much room." She patted the birth file that was on the desktop. "And I will make more desks out of ivory when I get my shipment back."

The woman with long black hair cut in. "Señora Günerro?"

"Yes?"

The woman now put her hand on Lucas's shoulder. "Lucas and I are so happy to be together again. And I want to thank you, Señora Günerro, for making this happen. You're too kind."

"It's the way most people see me," Ms. Günerro said.

"But I have a request," the woman said. "I was wondering if it's possible for me to work here in Las Vegas so I can be close to Lucas."

"You want a transfer?" Ms. Günerro said.

"Yes," the woman said.

Ms. Günerro popped a frozen pea in her mouth. "Since I am nice *and* I have Lucas's file, I'll honor your request, provided Lucas lives here in the Good Hotel."

Ms. Günerro stood and began walking up the flight of stairs behind her desk. "Let's do it now," she said. "Let's go visit the head of housekeeping and get you started right away cleaning some toilets."

The woman with long black hair said, "I thought our agreement was that I would be head of housekeeping for the Good Hotels in America."

"In due time," Ms. Günerro said. "In life, you have to work to get ahead."

Lucas and the woman with long black hair followed Ms. Günerro, and the six Curukian boys followed them to the lobby.

LOCKSMITH

The entrance of the Good Hotel Las Vegas was an underwater dreamland.

A giant marble fountain dominated the center of the room. Jets of water shot up to the ceiling and flowed through waves of blown glass and down the walls. It was like being underneath a giant wave.

This ocean theme repeated itself in the lobby with clamshell couches, lobster chairs, and starfish coffee tables. Someone dressed in scuba gear played a whale-shaped piano.

In her mermaid dress Ms. Günerro floated across the room toward the music. She shooed the piano player away, and he waddled out in flippers as Ms. Günerro placed the birth chart on the music rack and sat down.

Immediately Lucas recognized that she was playing Debussy's *La Mer*. It was a version that Lucas had to admit was much better than Mr. Siloti's at the New Resistance Hotel-School.

Lucas scanned the lobby for an exit.

Ekki and Goper were standing guard by the front doors, and Curukians with earpieces bunched together in clumps of three. Escape would be impossible. At least right now.

While Ms. Günerro was playing, the hotel manager approached in an all-white captain's uniform with shiny shoes and hat to match. A brass nameplate on his left breast-pocket flap read FRED ALFRED.

Parents couldn't come up with another name? Lucas thought.

"Mr. Alfred," Ms. Günerro said.

"Please call me Fred," Mr. Alfred said.

As Ms. Günerro played the piano, she gestured toward Lucas and the woman with long black hair. "This is Lucas Kapriss and his mother, Luz Kapriss. Cute—aren't they?"

"Cute as mice boogers," he said.

"As what?" Ms. Günerro asked, pausing her fingers on the keys for a second.

"It's an expression from back home," he said. "You see . . ."

"I don't care about your home," Ms. Günerro said.

"Oh, okay," Mr. Alfred said.

Ms. Günerro said, "Lucas is going to be my guest in the Good Suite."

"But it's—"

"Never mind that," Ms. Günerro said. "He is to remain under twenty-four-hour watch." Ms. Günerro pointed at the two closest Curukians. "Those two young men can stand outside the Good Suite today."

Ms. Günerro's started playing again and swiveled

toward a woman who had just walked up in a white uniform.

Without stopping the music, Ms. Günerro asked, "Are you head of housekeeping?"

"Yes, madam, I am Esmeralda."

"Were you the one who designed my desk downstairs?"

"Yes, madam," Esmeralda said.

"You'll be making me more desks very soon," Ms. Günerro said. She nodded toward the woman with long black hair. "But for the moment, I want Luz to start working at the Good Hotel Las Vegas immediately. Do whatever it is you do to have these cleaning people clean."

"I'll get her a cart right away," Esmeralda said as she scurried away.

Magnus came up and stood next to the manager.

"We have our container number," said Ms. Günerro glancing at the file folder.

"And," Magnus said, "Agent Janssens has already given us the dock information. I'll pull your car around. We have a flight to catch."

Just as he was leaving the lobby, two men wearing bright yellow jumpsuits and hats came in through the front door. The men eased over to the concierge desk.

"If I may ask," Mr. Alfred said to Ms. Günerro. "How long will Mr. Lucas Kapriss be staying with us in the Good Suite?"

Ms. Günerro pointed at the birth chart on the

music rack. "Until I finish reading this wonderful treasure trove that Lucas was so kind to return to me, which I will be reading on the flight."

"Very well," Mr. Alfred said.

"And," Ms. Günerro said, "as soon as I leave, call Interpol and let them know Lucas Kapriss is here. They may have him listed as Lucas Benes."

"Interpol?" Mr. Alfred asked. "The international police agency?"

"That one," Ms. Günerro replied. "Ask to be connected to Agent Charlotte Janssens."

"Yes," Mr. Alfred said. "Esmeralda and I will take care of everything."

Ms. Günerro turned back to the piano and began playing even louder.

As Esmeralda rejoined the group, Fred Alfred said to her, "I had no idea our CEO was this good on the piano."

"You stay here and listen," Esmeralda said. "I'll take Luz to the housekeeping room."

Mr. Alfred looked at Lucas and the two Curukians. "Esmeralda," he said. "Would you also take Lucas to the Good Suite? And these boys. They're supposed to guard the door or something."

"Certainly," she said.

Esmeralda led the way. The woman with long black hair followed, pushing the cleaning cart down the hallway, and the Curukians and Lucas trailed the two women.

CHAPTER TWENTY

As they walked away, the piano music faded.

Esmeralda whispered to Lucas. "Did you like Ms. Günerro's desk?"

"It was very nice, except for the elephant-tusk legs."

"I mean the desktop," she said.

"What about it?"

"Your mother taught me the pattern." Esmeralda stared straight through Lucas. "You understand me."

Lucas pulled up the picture of the desk in his mind. He saw the swirls. He saw the golden spiral. He remembered the number on the birth chart. Phi backward. They were all related.

Lucas smiled. "That's how I find the code hidden in the birth file, isn't it?"

Esmeralda nodded, and then she and the woman with long black hair turned down another hallway. The Curukians escorted Lucas to a set of double doors, where the taller boy opened the door to the Good Suite.

The other Curukian touched his index finger to the cord spiraling from his ear and spoke into his wrist microphone, "Good Suite guest now entering the secure location."

The boys pushed Lucas in and locked the door behind him. The room was nothing but an empty construction zone with white painter's tape on gray sheet rock. There was no bed, lamp, TV. Nothing. In the bathroom, there was a toilet and sink. The window was a thick pane of glass.

Lucas twisted the door handle, but it was locked from the outside.

It was more of a cell than a hotel room.

TIME TO CHECK OUT

Lucas knew the door was locked but tried the handle again.

One of the Curukians on the other side banged his fist on the jamb. "Cut it out!"

Through the peephole Lucas could see the woman with long black hair pushing a cleaning cart. He saw the two men in yellow. The lettering on their jumpsuits read LOST VEGAS LOCKSMITH.

Then he saw the briefcase.

Alister! Lucas couldn't believe it. The men were Alister and Jackknife!

Out of nowhere, Jackknife started cartwheeling down the hallway. The Brazilian was a flying tumbleweed of yellow.

Jackknife literally flew in midair toward the two Curukians.

A body at rest stays at rest unless acted upon by an external force.

In this case Jackknife was the external force as his feet nailed both boys, emptying their lungs and sending them to the floor.

One of the Curukians rolled over and moaned into

his wrist microphone, "Help!"

Lucas peered down through the peephole.

Alister was already opening the briefcase and hooking up the Kano computer to the key-card slot.

Blip, blip, and the door opened.

Lucas wanted to hug his buddies, but there was no time. Three new Curukians were racing toward them.

Lucas, Jackknife, and Alister ran toward the house-keeping cart at the end of the hallway. The woman with long black hair handed each boy two bottles of cleaning fluid.

Like gunslingers from the Wild West, the three boys held the spray bottles out in front of them and blasted the Curukians in the face with chemicals. In their eyes, in their mouths, on their earpieces. It wouldn't hurt them, but it would sting and stop them for a minute.

"Sorry," Lucas said. "But I meant to tell you that I needed to check out of my room a little early today."

UBER

Jackknife, Alister, and Lucas ducked into the stairwell.

Footsteps were coming from somewhere. At this point it could have been anyone. Curukians. Hotel security. Interpol. Or maybe just a guest staying in the Good Hotel.

"How did you guys get here?" Lucas asked.

"Uber," Jackknife said.

"But the driver's gone," Alister said.

"Follow me," Lucas said. "I'm your new Uber."

They raced down the stairs and blasted into the private garage.

"Whoa," Jackknife said, staring at the Tesla. "Look at this car!"

"Get in," Lucas said, as he hit the garage-door opener on the wall.

The giant metal door scrolled upward. Light poured into the garage, and Lucas climbed into the driver's seat.

"Do you even know how to drive?" Alister said.

"I drove a bus in Paris," Lucas said defensively.

"You wrecked it into a river!" Jackknife said.

"Günerro did."

"Guys," Alister said.

The interior was smooth black leather. Lucas could barely see over the steering wheel, so he ratcheted the seat forward.

Jackknife hopped in the passenger seat while Alister and his briefcase climbed into the back.

Lucas started the engine and slowly and quietly rolled out of the garage.

Goper and Ekki rounded the corner of the hotel on Segways, tiny blue lights flashing on their helmets. In the side-view mirrors Lucas could see the two guards zeroing in on the Tesla. He put his finger over the control panel and tapped INSANE. In 3.2 seconds the speedometer hit one hundred kilometers per hour, and the car rocketed across the parking lot and into the streets of Las Vegas.

As they passed the Bellagio fountains, Lucas buzzed the windows down. A Frank Sinatra song boomed from the fountain that shot geysers of water seventy-three meters up into the desert air.

After two more corners, Lucas nosed the Tesla around the parked cars and stopped right in front of the valet station at the Globe Hotel.

Astrid was waiting on the sidewalk with her arms folded.

Jackknife said, "I think we're in trouble."

IT'S TIME

Astrid shook her head as Lucas, Jackknife, and Alister climbed out of the Tesla.

"You guys are in trouble," she said.

"Magnus kidnapped me in this car," Lucas said. "I just drove it back."

"It's not that," Astrid said. "Someone broke into the file room."

"Hmmm," Jackknife mused. "Wonder who that could have been?"

Alister glanced at his yellow jumpsuit. "Haven't got the foggiest idea," he said.

"I don't want to know how you got in there," Astrid said. "But keep your mouths shut and change out of those ridiculous theater costumes. The fact that the emblem says 'Lost Vegas Locksmith' might be a dead giveaway."

Alister and Jackknife unzipped the jumpsuits. Underneath they were wearing the clothes they had had on earlier. Alister still had his bow tie on, and Jackknife wore his Pelé shirt. Lucas gave the keys and the jumpsuits to the valet, and they followed Astrid through the hotel and down to the

New Resistance Hotel-School.

When they passed the principal's office, Lucas peered through the blinds and spotted Big Mac sitting in front of her desk with his head in his hands.

Dr. Kloppers scurried over to the door. "Were you two boys out of bounds today at lunchtime by any chance?"

Astrid cranked up her inner lawyer. "I haven't had time to discuss this matter with my clients."

"It's a simple question, Astrid," Dr. Kloppers said. "I think the boys can answer for themselves." The head of school gestured toward Big Mac in her office. "Mr. MacDonald here said he saw Lucas and Alister breaking into the file room today during lunch."

"If that were true," Astrid said, "if Mr. MacDonald did in fact see my clients, Alister and Lucas, then he, too, would have been out of bounds. And if so, then his testimony would be—"

"Enough," Dr. Kloppers said. "You've made your point, young lady."

Astrid, Lucas, Jackknife, and Alister headed to the Grotto for early dinner. The lights had been dimmed, which picked up an orange tint in the rock walls. The sugary smell of doughnut glaze still hung in the air, even though the cooks were already putting hot steaming pans into the buffet counter.

The café was about half full. Travis was sitting in a booth with Walter, who was sound asleep. Nalini was playing with Gini and talking with Zibby about how to babysit. Lucas sort of missed the little kid in a big-brother kind of way. Gini had helped them so much in Paris, and now it seemed everyone wanted to take care of her. Especially Nalini, who had somehow overnight become an expert on mothering.

Astrid, Lucas, Jackknife, and Alister went through the line and got their dinner trays. A few minutes later Mr. Benes walked straight up to their table. Lucas swallowed hard.

"I heard there was a problem over at the Good Hotel today," he said calmly. "What do you know about this Lucas?"

"Dad?"

"Yes?"

"You know that woman that Magnus went to the airport with?"

"Yes."

"Well, I met her today," Lucas said. "Like you said, she's not my mother, but she told me what happened to her, and how Bunguu's diamonds actually belonged to my grandfather."

"So the legend of the Kapriss diamonds lives on," Mr. Benes said.

"You know about this?"

"Madame Beach has always believed there were dark secrets hidden in the Good Company." Mr. Benes said. "Did this woman you met today tell you how to interpret your birth chart?"

Lucas put his fork down and thought for a second.

He had tons of new clues.

"According to Alister, my mother left a ridiculously complex algorithm in the file."

"Can you figure it out?"

"I think I can, but I'll need help."

Mr. Benes took a phone from his inside coat pocket. "Etta," he said into the microphone. "It's time."

EMERGENCY MEETING

The sound of Etta Kerr's soft British voice came across the school's intercom system.

"Attention," the communications director announced. "This announcement is an official Call to Legs. All Tier One and Two students report to the main boardroom for an emergency meeting."

Lucas and the others trailed Mr. Benes from the Grotto and across the cavern in fire-drill silence. Other kids were streaming down the sidewalks. No one was talking. There had never been an emergency meeting at night. Ever.

Emerald, who normally worked as a flight attendant, held the door open.

A dark wooden table surrounded by office chairs occupied the center of the room. The fifth-year seniors in high school, Robbie Stafford from Australia and Sophia Carson from New Zealand, sat at the far end without smiling. Behind them was a giant monitor that showed the NRHS logo. On the sides of the room there were rows of carrels for Tier Two team members.

Coach Creed was standing in the kitchen area off

to the side, drinking coffee. He was wearing sport shorts and a T-shirt that read CAFÉ CAFFÈ CAFÉ.

His enormous voice filled the room. "Good evening, everybody. Let's get your tails a-moving and put them in a seat."

Lucas sat at the Tier One table with Travis, Jack-knife, Astrid, and Nalini and Gini. Everyone else took seats on the sides.

"What's this all about?" Mac said.

"Why don't you wait a second," Astrid said, "instead of starting out being annoying."

Mac took a carrel opposite Astrid. "I don't even know why we're doing any of this," he said. "We're a bunch of kids in a boardroom. Doesn't anybody else think this is kind of stupid?"

"You stupid," Gini said.

"That proves my point," Mac said. "You've got this baby that supposedly helped you in Paris, and you're toting her around like some good-luck charm."

"Mac," Kerala said from a carrel across the room. "I am a polyglot, which means I can speak a lot of languages, but I don't much like to talk in general. I used to think this whole New Resistance stuff was kind of hokey too. I'll have to admit—kids solving problems created by adults? Really? But when we were in Paris, I saw how Lucas's *inexperience* actually helped us."

"Inexperience is a weakness," Mac argued back.

Astrid fidgeted like she was itching to get in on

the argument. "Kerala's right," she said. "The fact that Lucas and the rest of us didn't have some fixed idea of how things were supposed to work out actually made him and all of us come up with new and creative ideas, and we saved a bunch of kids."

"We're adaptable," said Jackknife.

"Listen here, Mac," Coach Creed said. "Any numbskull can complain. In this school, we express ourselves by our likes rather than our dislikes. If you want to join our program, you'll need to rewire your thoughts."

Coach Creed always had a way of ending a discussion. Everyone sat silent for about five seconds.

"Coach Creed?" Mr. Benes asked. "I have a feeling we're going to need an airplane tonight. Will you kindly make sure White Bird One is ready to go?"

"Will do," he said, and left the room.

Mr. Benes sat on a stool in the kitchen area. "Robbie, you ready?"

Robbie nodded. "Okay," he said. "Normally at this point we know where we're going, and we would decide who should go where. But we still have heaps of work to do."

Sophia leaned her head toward Robbie and whispered something. They both looked at Lucas.

"Lucas," Robbie said. "Why don't you get us up to speed on what you know?"

"I think starting at the end might be better," Lucas said. "I know we'll end up at my birth chart."

"Where is it now?" Robbie asked.

"It's in Alister's briefcase."

Mac shouted out. "Because you stole it."

"Terry," Robbie said, "would you please take Lucas's birth chart into the tech room and upload a digital version to the cloud."

Terry took the file and left the room.

"Maybe," Sophia said, "you should start at the beginning. And we'll see if we've missed something along the way."

Everyone leaned forward, fascinated—like Lucas was about to reveal a big secret.

THE LEGEND MUST BE TRUE

Lucas cleared his throat.

"Earlier today," he explained, "I met a woman with long black hair who was supposed to be my mother. Turns out she was an impostor, but she's secretly helping us."

Everyone was listening. Lily Hill and some Tier Two kids were taking notes.

"The big thing I learned was my mother really was killed by the Good Company."

There was collective gasp of shock, but still no one spoke.

"I was pretty sure of that already," Lucas said, glancing back at his dad. "But this woman also told me that my mother was part of a team of hotel house-keepers who were and are trying to expose the Good Company for what they really are."

With the exception of the Tier Two kids who were typing, all eyes were on Lucas.

"I also found out that my grandfather used to own a diamond mine in the Belgian Congo." He paused. "But some people in the Congolese army didn't like foreigners. There was a group led by General

Bunguu, Lu Bunguu's father, who overthrew the government and took over the mine. Then, with money and diamonds stolen from my grandfather, the Bunguu family and the Günerro family started the Good Company."

The kids moaned at hearing this awful news.

Several kids blurted out, "What!"

"No way!"

"Unbelievable," Jackknife said, pounding his fist on the table.

"Wait a minute!" Astrid said. "If the Bunguu and Günerro families started the Good Company together, how is that Ms. Günerro now works for Lu Bunguu?"

Mr. Benes set a coffee cup down and spoke up. "We've heard a version of this story for years," he said. "I don't think it is a question of who works for whom with Bunguu and Günerro. It's more a question of how they can help each other make more money."

Everyone got quiet again as they waited for the next piece of information.

"Alister," Lucas said, "probably knows more about this than anybody."

Sophia asked, "How so?"

"Alister's father knew my mother," Lucas said.

The dots on Alister's cheeks reddened as everyone turned to him. He set his briefcase up on his carrel.

"About twelve years ago, Lu Bunguu sent a shipping container to the Good Hotel Buenos Aires,"

Alister explained. "Lucas's mother, as head of house-keeping, opened it and found her father's diamonds, as well as tons of ivory, gold, and cash."

Travis gasped. He seemed struck with an idea, and he buried his head in his computer.

"Go on, Alister," Robbie said.

"Lucas's mother deposited the money in my father's bank in the Falklands." He paused. "And she gave him specific instructions on what to do with the container of diamonds, gold, and ivory."

Robbie asked excitedly, "Is FLK in Lucas's birth chart an abbreviation for the Falklands?"

"It is," Alister said. "FLK is the ISO code for the Falkland Islands."

"What about the ivory?" Sophia asked. "Do you mean elephant tusks?"

Someone in Tier Two typed into his computer, and in a second the screen behind Sophia filled with images of ivory tusks being confiscated by the police.

"Literally a ton," Alister said. "Two thousand pounds. Nine hundred and seven kilograms of ivory tusks to be exact."

"If your father shipped this container away," Astrid asked, "then *to where* did he ship it?"

"I don't know," Alister said. "What you have to understand is that Lucas's mother was a maths wiz of some kind." His Scottish accent seemed heightened, and he pronounced *math* with an *s* at the end. "Using a complex set of instructions, she sent the container to different Good Hotels all over the world. My father paid for everything using Bunguu's stolen money."

"Stolen from Lucas's grandfather!" Jackknife pointed out.

Alister stopped like he had nothing more to say. He looked to Lucas, who was also speechless.

"Great," Mac said. "Alister knows as much as Lucas does, which is nothing."

"You nuthin'," Gini said.

The way Mac had accused Lucas and Alister allowed the other kids to call out freely. A burst of worried gossip filled the room.

Li Ha, the new Chinese girl, said, "Mac has a point here."

Her roommate, Emma, added, "We don't know anything more than that the letters *FLK* mean the Falklands?"

Mac seemed to like the breakdown, and he kept antagonizing the group. "This is a big waste of time."

"Wait a minute," Travis said. "These are Kapriss diamonds!"

Sophia asked, "Other than having Lucas's middle name, what's special about these diamonds as opposed to regular ones?"

"Kapriss diamonds are first-rate," Travis explained. "The best of the best. And no one cuts them like this anymore, which makes them extremely valuable. Some are worth a million dollars apiece!"

Someone in Tier Two said, "And that's why Ms.

Günerro would want them. They're the best."

Travis glanced at a page on his screen. "Now the diamonds coming out of Bunguu's mine are of poor quality, and he's run the place down. The profits all go to pay for wars and child soldiers."

"Children," Nalini said, holding Gini up, "who could have been trafficked like this."

"The legend must be true," Mr. Benes said. "Ms. Günerro wants these diamonds, not just because they're worth a fortune. But if the police find Kapriss diamonds, then they'll connect the Good Company with the Bunguu family, and that would be not only devastating but could land her in jail."

The room went dead silent.

Mr. Benes said, "Alister, I want you up here with Tier One."

The Falklander sheepishly moved across the room and sat next to Lucas. He set his briefcase on the floor.

"So," Robbie said, putting his fingertips on the table. "Where do we find this container?"

Big Mac sulked. "I bet the Good Company knows where to go."

"No!" Lucas blurted. "They couldn't know."

Sophia said, "Why exactly?"

"Because they don't know the pattern," Lucas said.

The room went silent again.

"What pattern?" Sophia asked.

"The pattern is a map," Lucas said. "It's a route that

the container has taken over the last twelve years."

"Well," said Sophia, "where's the map?"

"It's hidden in my birth chart."

MAP VS. APP

The boardroom door opened, and Terry Hines rushed back in.

"The digital version of Lucas's birth chart is on the New Resistance cloud," he said. "Everyone should have access in their reading apps."

Robbie then called out orders, fast and methodical.

"Li Ha," he said. "Your dad was in shipping. Get me some data on all vessels that could potentially carry a container like this."

"Something else I learned today," Lucas said. "Supposedly this container only went to Good Hotels that are located on the sea or ocean."

Robbie stood. "Astrid! You work with Emma," he said, pointing toward the new German girl. "Get me the location of all Good Hotels near or on the water."

He looked to Sophia. "Let's get all this on screen one."

Astrid hopped up and went to work with Emma.

Robbie raised his arms and pointed toward the left side of the room. "Sora Kowa," he said to the Japanese girl. "Pull up every code in the file."

He pointed at Kerala, who looked asleep behind

her Goth makeup. "Kerala!" She raised her white face. "Scan Lucas's file for languages and see if you can come up with something."

The sound of keyboards clacking filled the room with a buzz.

Robbie didn't stop. "Jackknife?"

"Yeah."

"You grew up in São Paulo near the port, right?" he asked.

"Yeah," said Jackknife. "Number one port in South America."

"Perfect! Tier Two right side," Robbie called out. "I need the port authority in every city where there is a Good Hotel. Jackknife, you lead the port study."

"Let's go, Emma and Astrid," Robbie said. "We need that data now!"

Someone yelled across the room "What's the longitude and latitude of the Falklands?"

The room was a flurry of activity.

Robbie turned to Lucas. "What else?"

"There is a golden spiral on Ms. Günerro's desk," Lucas said. "It's part of a number, phi, one point six one eight zero three three, and relates to the Fibonacci sequence."

"Nalini," Robbie said, "you work with Zibby on the number phi and see if there's a relationship to make codes from. And Gini, too."

Mac bellowed from the back corner. "You're just making stuff up!"

"Stuff it," Gini said.

Terry Hines looked around.

"Whoa!" he said. "What did I miss while I was gone? I am so lost."

Melissa Rathbone called out, "The number one point six one is the ratio that relates the numbers in the Fibonacci sequence. Is there a relationship between the number and the location of the container or the hotel?"

"Oh," Terry said sarcastically, "now I get it. Not."

Lucas wasn't sure this was going to work. And he needed time to think. Alone.

"Ms. Günerro wouldn't use Fibonacci because it's not original," Travis said. "That's what Hervé, the French guy, told us at Notre Dame."

"Exactly why Lucas's mother would use it," Jack-knife said.

Sophia said, "Travis, would you explain the Fibonacci sequence?"

Lucas didn't listen. He knew this was a total fail.

"It's easy," Travis said. "Start with one plus one, which of course equals two, and one plus two equals three, two plus three is five, and so on. So your list looks like one, one, two, three, five, eight, thirteen . . .

"Turns out the ratio between each number after the first two is 1.6. Weird how that works out, but it does."

He paused to see if anyone was paying attention. Sophia and Robbie seemed to be the only ones listening.

"Just what I wanted," Mac said. "More math."

"Kerala," Sophia asked, "do you have any first impressions?"

Despite the black makeup, Kerala looked happy to be working. She perked up in her chair. "I have come up with at least thirty different languages in Lucas's chart. Nice Esperanto your dad writes, Alister."

"What do the languages tell you?" Sophia asked.

"Well," Kerala sighed. "Not really sure. At first the number fifty-one comes up a lot, but mostly it seems very random."

"Fifty-one," said a Tier Two kid, "is the country code for Peru."

"There's a Good Hotel in Lima," Emma said.

"Page three has PVR on it eight times," Kerala said. "It's diagonal and vertical on the page, with no clear meaning."

"PVR," Melissa Rathbone blurted out, "is the airport code for Puerto Vallarta, Mexico, isn't it?"

Emma confirmed this. "There's a Good Hotel there, too."

"Okay," Astrid announced. "We have the map ready."

Sophia pointed at the screen behind her. "Put it up here."

The room got a little quieter as the map appeared on the big monitor. It was a political world map with blue oceans and each country outlined in a different color.

Astrid explained. "Ms. Günerro and the Good Company own just under twelve hundred hotels worldwide."

Tiny red lights lit up the map.

"Of those, Emma and I have identified three hundred thirty-seven on a large body of water. Here they are."

The 337 lights blinked.

Robbie stood at the map. "So the container is in one of these three hundred thirty-seven hotels. Is this right, Lucas?"

Lucas bit his bottom lip. "Yeah," he said, studying the map. "I guess."

"By the time you find this container," Mac said, "it'll be gone."

The bubble of energy burst. Everyone turned to Mac.

"This container you're trying to find is old, right?"

"Twelve years old," Alister said.

Mac said, "All international shipping containers have to have a four-letter code ending in *U*, and they have to be registered with the BIC." He paused. "Now Lucas's mom may have been a math genius, and you may be able to figure out her complicated algorithm that she left in the birth file. But today we do have things called apps that speed things up a bit."

Still no one said anything.

"It's simple," he said. "Find the number and plug it into the website or on your phone. Not you, Lucas, you're too *cool* to have a smartphone. In a few seconds we'll know the location of the container."

Robbie asked, "Do we have the container number?"

"It's more than that," Mac said. "The first three letters are the owner's or shipper's code plus the letter *U* for this type of container."

"Then what?" Sophia asked.

"Six numbers," Mac said. "Plus a check number at the end."

"We have that number," Alister said. "It's got to be Lucas's birth chart number."

Lucas said, "Three three zero eight one six dash one."

"Okay," Robbie said. "But we don't know the owner's code."

"All you need to do," Mac said, "is figure out three letters that Lucas's mother or Alister's father would have used as their shipper's code."

"FLK?" Terry called out.

Astrid asked, "What about the Globe Hotel, TGH?"

"How about this," Robbie said. "Everyone go online right now and look up a container-tracking website. Input three letters from the chart plus the letter U plus three three zero eight one six dash one."

It was like someone had started a timer on a standardized test. The room fell into silence, and the kids dove into their work.

"Container not found," Emma called out, "on China Shipping."

"I'm getting the same thing," Sora Kowa said.

"Try LKBU."

"Container not found," Lily Hill said, "on Maersk."

"Keep trying other shippers," Robbie called out.

A few minutes later, Mr. Benes spoke up. "Twelve years ago we had just named our philanthropy group: The New Resistance," he said. "Try TNR."

Mac entered it into his app. "Container TNRU three three zero eight one six dash one arrived five nights ago at 19:07 in Civitavecchia, the port about an hour northwest of Rome, Italy. It was reloaded this morning at 5:04 onto a Hamburg Süd ship called the *Leviathan*. It sets sail tomorrow night at 20:27."

"Where's the ship headed?" Robbie asked.

"Barcelona."

"All right!" Terry Hines said as he clapped. "Barça—greatest *fútbol* team in the world."

Jackknife shot out of his seat. "What!" he said. "Brazil dominates."

Astrid cut them off. "Guys," she said. "Not right now!"

Mr. Benes said, "Sophia?"

"I know what you're going to ask," she said. "It's already done. We have an H1 heated and cooled bunk-sleeper container for seven people," she said. "We just actually have to get Tier One inside that container before they load it onto the ship."

"Okay," Mr. Benes said. "I want to make a few changes to the Tier One team." He paused to make sure everyone was listening.

"Nalini, since you're taking care of Gini, I want you to stay with us on the plane all the way to Barcelona. Kerala, I want you in on this mission since you speak Italian."

Mr. Benes pointed at Alister and Mac. "You two have proven yourselves today. I want you both on Tier One. Let's go."

The Boeing 747 Intercontinental airliner was waiting.

Techs were streaming all over the place getting White Bird One ready. There were fire and fuel trucks, baggage handlers loading boxes onto conveyor belts, and security patrolling on mountain bikes.

The seats were ultramodern, oversize pods tricked out with everything, so it didn't really matter which place you got. Everyone in the New Resistance flew first class.

Etta came over the speaker.

"Thanks so much for riding with us today, kids!" she said in her cheery voice. "Take a seat pod, buckle those belts, and do have a pleasant day as we head over to Rome, Italy."

INTERPOL

In the center of Lyon, France, nestled alongside the Parc de la Tête d'Or, Agent Charlotte Janssens sat alone in her Interpol office. The walls were gray, and the furniture was made of French oak. A new computer sat on her desk, and next to the keyboard stood an empty cup of coffee.

Agent Janssens placed her newly manicured nails on the keyboard and opened up a secure email.

She typed:

Lyon, FRANCE – Interpol is calling on all police departments and border-patrol agents to track an international fugitive. Parisian police discovered fingerprints on the steering wheel of a bus that sank last month in the river Seine. The prints belong to the following:

Present family name: Benes
Forename: Lucas Kapriss
Nationality: Argentina/USA
Age today: 14 years old

Intelligence believes the fugitive to be residing in Nevada, USA. Recent leads indicate that Mr. Lucas Benes may have travel plans in or around Rome, Italy. If found, do not apprehend. Report back to me directly.

Current American passport picture included with the attached bulletin.

Agent Charlotte Janssens
Interpol Special Operations

Agent Janssens hit send. Then she went for a walk in the park.

PASSAPORTO

The sound of Etta's voice came across the airplane's intercom system. "Good morning," she said softly. "We arrive in Rome in thirty minutes."

Scattered across his brain Lucas could see fragments of a dream floating away. He reached into the back of his mind and snatched whatever pieces he could hang on to. During the flight that night he had dreamed of containers filled with his grandfather's diamonds. He wondered if uncovering something from his past would lead him toward his future.

Lucas stayed in his pod thinking for a minute until it hit him. You can't let your family—past or present, living or dead, rich or poor—define who you are now.

The automatic door to the main cabin slid open. Robbie and Sophia followed Emerald pushing a cart down the aisle, passing out euros for spending money.

"Good morning," Sophia said. "I hope everyone's ready."

"The plan looks like this," Robbie said. "We'll drop you off here in Rome at a private airstrip. While we refuel the plane, you'll have to go into the small passport office. After that you'll board the bus that's waiting and go straight to Civitavecchia, where you'll set up shop in our converted container."

"Unfortunately," Sophia said, "there is no touring around Rome today."

No one said anything. It was too early in the day to talk.

Sophia handed Astrid an envelope. "Inside you'll find a credit card for emergencies. And there's a phone that will work on the open seas."

Robbie added, "Once you find the phi container, text us, and we'll wrap this mission up. We have teams in Malta, Sicily, and Corsica waiting for your message."

White Bird One landed at a private airstrip attached to the Ciampino Airport near Rome.

The new Tier One—Lucas, Astrid, Jackknife, Travis, Kerala, Alister, and Mac—descended the flight of stairs and walked across the tarmac toward a small, white trailer on wheels. A block of wooden steps led up to a metal door. A multi-language sign said it was the passport, immigration, and border-patrol office.

Mac held the door for everyone but kept his eyes on White Bird One, now being refueled.

Opera music blared from inside the trailer.

"That's Puccini," Astrid said over the music. "But Kerala, could you ask the guy to kill the sound?"

Kerala spoke to the man, and he turned the volume down.

The metal building was furnished with one chair

and a fold-up table. The passport officer sat behind this desk, which was littered with stacks of papers and forms, a laptop, and handheld stamping machines.

Tacked on the bulletin board behind the table were posters about work safety and smaller printed sheets with pictures of people from different countries.

"Passaporti," the agent said to everyone.

The New Resistance kids lined up and took out their passports. Lucas had two valid passports on him: an Argentinean one with an old picture and a brand-new one from the USA. He chose to show his American passport since it had no stamps in it.

Kerala went first in line and chatted with the officer for a second. As the man stamped each of the kids' passports, he glanced up at them, presumably to see if the photograph and the person matched.

While he waited, Lucas scanned the bulletin board behind the desk. His eyes flicked back and forth past the pictures of international fugitives. Row by row Lucas memorized them, trying to see if he recognized anyone. Then he spotted a picture he knew well. The same picture that was in his American passport was staring right back at him.

"Passaporto," the agent said to Lucas.

Lucas's heart jumped into his throat. He jammed the American passport into his back pocket, patted his chest and pants, and then pulled out his old Argentinean passport.

"Molto vecchio," the man said, inspecting the

exterior of the beaten-up passport. Then in labored English he said, "Very old."

Lucas could feel his face getting flush like when he didn't have his homework done and got called on in class. He was sure his face was bright red. Guilty as charged.

The man slowly flipped through the booklet and stared at every single page. There was hardly room for another stamp. With the turn of each page Lucas could feel sweat gathering in his armpits.

The man's unibrow furrowed. "I know you."

Lucas gulped.

"You are famous? No?"

Lucas shrugged and shook his head. He didn't want to call attention to the Interpol poster sitting right behind the guy.

"Where are you going in Italy?" the officer asked with a smile.

Travis whispered to the others. "If we don't tell the guy what we're doing, he'll stop us here."

"I agree," Astrid said, nodding toward Kerala. "Tell him that we're supposed to catch a ship across the Mediterranean to Barcelona."

Kerala told the man what they were doing, and the officer typed into his computer. He leaned back in his chair and waved good-bye.

"*Ciao,*" he said.

"*Ciao,*" they replied.

The tour bus was a brand-new Volvo 9900 and was freezing cold with air-conditioning. Lucas thought it was a perfect environment for jet-lag napping. But with black lights, plush couches, and video games it was also a playground. Behind a big monitor at the back, there was a minibar stocked with snacks and drinks, and a door with the word *toilet* written in ten languages. Lucas crashed into the center couch next to Alister, where they compared their white teeth in the black lights.

The driver steered the bus across the tarmac and through a security gate and into the town. A traffic jam clogged the first intersection. The driver joined the others stuck in traffic by banging on his horn.

Travis and Astrid started playing a video game, and Mac and Kerala watched. Jackknife got up and went to the bathroom. From inside the little room, someone moaned.

"Hey!" he called out. "This door is locked. And there's someone in here!"

GLAD TO BE GLADIATORS

Siba Günerro put on a pair of cat-eye sunglasses as she stepped out onto the balcony of the Good Hotel Rome. She popped a frozen pea in her mouth as she surveyed the Vatican below.

The CEO of the Good Company wore a white suit with tails of gossamer fabric that drifted in the wind. To the north, Ms. Günerro spied her helicopter returning to its base. Then she dipped her glasses to watch the storm clouds that were gathering over the greater Mediterranean Sea.

Behind her, Charles Magnus was talking on the phone.

"Yes, Charlotte," he said. "I printed out your email. I'll give it to her now."

He hung up and handed Ms. Günerro a piece of paper. She read:

For Interpol eyes only:
Private jet White Bird One landed thirty minutes ago at an airstrip at the Ciampino Airport. Local passport agent reports the following passengers entering Italy: Kerala Dresden, Paulo Cabral, Astrid Benes, Travis

Chase, Mac MacDonald, Alister Thanthalon Laramie Nethington IV, and Lucas Benes.

The passport agent on duty said that he did not recall receiving the bulletin prior to the fugitive's arrival. The group is departing by ship from Civitavecchia at 20:27 local time.

Ms. Günerro said, "The passport agent is obviously lying or he's just a buffoon. He didn't release the New Resistance kids. They got away."

"Doubtful," Magnus said.

"Why?" Ms. Günerro asked. "Where are they now?"

"On a bus."

"And who's driving?"

"Let's put it this way," Magnus said. "It's not the original driver."

Ms. Günerro said, "The New Resistance is full of weaselly little brats—like all children, they're slimy and will slip out the first chance they have."

"You're right."

"I'm always right!" she said. "If they do get away, they'll probably try to get to Civitavecchia through Roma Termini. Put some Curukians at the station and have them follow Lucas if he shows up."

"Certainly," Magnus said. "We have two guards who are training at the Roman Gladiator School." He nodded. "They would be happy to use their newly learned skills."

"You mean," Ms. Günerro said, chuckling, "they would be glad to be gladiators!"

ALL ROADS LEAD TO ROME

The expression "All roads lead to Rome" didn't literally have to mean "roads." It simply could mean that there was more than one way of getting into the city. One could get to Rome by boat or plane or on roads of iron.

The bus driver laid on the horn again, protesting the traffic jam.

Alister flipped open his briefcase and inserted what looked like an ice pick into a hole in the door handle of the toilet room.

"Give me the credit card," he said.

Astrid handed it to him, and Alister slid the card between the door and jamb. He wiggled the lock, and the door clicked open.

A small stocky man tied in a ball on the floor spilled out of the room and into the aisle. His short-sleeve shirt was torn, and his hands and feet were lashed with sisal ropes. A giant piece of duct tape covered his face from ear to ear. Lucas untied the knots while Jackknife gently peeled the tape from the man's mouth.

He looked up at the kids standing over him. "Get off the bus," he said. "While you still can."

When the phony bus driver saw what was happening in the rearview mirror, he ratcheted up the emergency brake, locked the doors, and barged down the aisle.

Travis, Jackknife, Kerala, and Mac clustered around the driver, blocking him between the couches.

"Give me a soft drink," Astrid said to Lucas.

He opened the minifridge and tossed her a can of Chinotto.

"Duck!" Astrid yelled.

The others dropped.

Astrid hurled the drink across the bus. The driver turned to miss it, but the spinning soda can smacked him above the eyebrows. The man howled and fell back onto a couch, squeezing the gash on his forehead.

Jackknife grabbed hold of two handrails, and in one swift swinging motion, he catapulted his feet into the locked doors. They nearly blasted off their hinges as they snapped open.

"Which way, Map Boy?" Astrid said as they hit the sidewalk.

When Lucas was in fifth grade he had built a diorama of Rome for his inquiry project. He had memorized practically every street and aqueduct in modern and ancient Rome. He closed his eyes for a half second, and multiple maps of Rome and its environs filled his head.

The group only made it three steps before the phony driver stumbled into the road after them, blood pouring into his eyes. The real driver leaped off the stalled bus after him and tackled the man to the street, where they fell into a brawl.

With a slight whistle Lucas started up the sidewalk, motioning the others to follow.

Lucas, Astrid, Jackknife, Travis, Kerala, and Alister snaked through the town toward the train station. When they got to the piazza, they spotted a triangle of policemen gathering outside. They were checking everyone and letting one person through the gate at a time. The fact that policemen were guarding the entrance killed the idea of leaving by train. They might have seen Lucas's picture in the Interpol bulletin.

Sometimes it wasn't skill or knowledge that made you succeed in life. Sometimes it was sheer determination. Lucas had to get to the port and get on that ship and find the container that his mother had diverted from the Good Company.

He whipped around and headed back the way they had come. Mac MacDonald was panting up the road toward them, his feet slapping the ground and making a noise the police could probably hear. Lucas signaled him to follow. The rest of the kids trailed Lucas as he hurried to the next intersection, where they saw another police checkpoint.

"Everything is blocked!" Travis said.

Mac threw his hands up in the air. "We're not going to outrun the Roman police—they have Lamborghinis."

"You're right, Mac, we won't outrun them," Lucas

said, "but Lamborghinis have to drive on roads."

Another map formed in Lucas's head, and he took off down the street. A minute later they were in a parking lot strewn with wooden crates and beat-up cars. They jogged up a tiny ramp that led straight to the train tracks.

"You can't go that way," Astrid said even before Lucas had said anything.

"Like they say, 'All roads lead to Rome,'" Lucas said. "Even roads of iron."

Astrid planted her hands on her hips. "We could get hit by a train."

"These tracks will take us to the station on the other side of this police blockade. From there we can catch a commuter train. We've got to go through Roma Termini—it's now the best way for us to get to the port."

Before Lucas could make a move, the ground began to shake. Within twenty seconds a white commuter train bombed past them, blowing everyone back.

"Sorry," he said to Astrid. "That would've been ugly."

She nodded, accepting his apology.

Lucas looked both ways down the train track. "But now we have ten minutes before another train comes."

They raced down the tracks and arrived at the Capannelle station, where Astrid got the credit card back from Alister and bought tickets. They boarded the next commuter train into Rome.

The plan was simple. They would go to Roma Termini—the end of the line. There, they would get on the express train that would take them out to the port. They would have tons of time to spare before getting on the ship.

It was thirteen minutes before they arrived at the main train station in Rome.

GLADIATOR SCHOOL?

As one of the oldest continuously occupied cities in Europe, Rome was often called the Eternal City. The capital of Italy was killer (as in an awesome place to visit), but it was once considered killer (as in deadly) if gladiators just so happened to want you dead.

Lucas had no intention of dying in Rome or spending an eternity there.

But when they stepped onto the platform, they spotted an unexpected pair of gladiators wearing traditional tunics with flowing red capes and gold helmets. They had silver swords and shields at their sides. One of the fighters stepped forward, his blond curly locks poking out the back of his helmet.

What? thought Lucas. *It's Goper Bradus!*

The other gladiator flicked open his visor, and Ekki Ellwoode Ekki's round eyeglasses stared out.

As the kids moved toward the men, Astrid fired off the first question. "What are you two doing here?"

"Duh," Ekki said, pointing to his outfit. "We're gladiators!"

"We can see that," Travis said. "But aren't you off by a few thousand years?"

Goper said, "There's a gladiator school in Rome and we're here to learn."

"Yeah," Ekki added, "it's called education."

"So what exactly are you learning to do?" Mac asked.

"Capture seven kids while wearing heavy armor?" Alister asked.

"No," Goper said. "We just want to follow you."

"Yeah," Ekki said. "Lucas tricked Ms. Günerro with the wrong birth chart."

Astrid asked, "You're going to follow us in those ridiculous outfits?"

"Good luck," Jackknife said.

Astrid moved to the kiosk and bought tickets for everyone. Lucas snatched the credit card from the machine before she could pocket it.

"I'll need it," Lucas whispered.

"Why?"

"I'm not going with you on the next train."

"Why not?"

"These guys are here for me, and I should have no problem outrunning them in those costumes!"

"That's crazy," Mac said.

"I know this city better than those two clowns," Lucas said.

Kerala poked into the conversation. "But," she said, "you've never been here before. I have."

"I've got the city map in my head," Lucas said.

"That could work," Astrid said. "We'll go to the port and do the paperwork for our container, and we'll meet you there before they load us up."

"I've fled this city before," Kerala said. "I'm coming with you."

WHEN IN ROME

Kerala's tone was so emphatic that Lucas couldn't help but give in.

They left the others and headed into the main train station. The open area was crowded with travelers carrying suitcases and shoppers toting bags and pickpockets looking for distracted people.

Goper and Ekki followed in their clanging metal costumes.

Kerala and Lucas cut through the crowds into the shopping mall of Roma Termini. They moved quickly, but when Lucas glanced back, he saw Goper and Ekki still keeping pace.

Outside they stepped into a blazing hot afternoon filled with smog and sirens. Lucas and Kerala cut between the rows of white taxis and ran across the crosswalk.

A white van with no side windows passed in front of them. Small satellite dishes shaped like a human ear and eyeball slowly spun on top of the vehicle's roof. In Italian and in English, the logo and tagline on the sides of the van said it all:

GOOD COMPANY IMAGES
WATCHING AND LISTENING
SO YOU DON'T HAVE TO

Lucas's eyes followed the van down the street until he lost it in the traffic circle.

Lucas and Kerala headed up the piazza dei Cinquecento, under the pine trees, and past the green-white-and-red Italian flags flapping in the breeze, where they stopped in the shade of a tour bus.

Kerala's black Goth makeup was starting to bleed. "So what's the plan?" she asked. "Run through Rome until we lose these ridiculous-looking gladiators?"

"They're just following us. Goper doesn't want to hurt us. He's just doing what someone told him to do."

"There will be Curukians looking for us too," Kerala said. "And there is only one real way to move through Rome at any speed."

Lucas looked right into Kerala's eyes. She totally understood what they were doing. The best way to get away from these guys was not to run but to ride.

"You're right," Lucas said. "See those palm trees? That's the Baths of Diocletian. So that means there should be a Bici and Baci rental shop right down here to the left."

Lucas stopped.

"What?" Kerala asked.

"I don't have a license to rent a moped."

"No worries," Kerala said. "I have fake IDs and driver's

licenses for five different countries."

Outside the store there were hundreds of mopeds backed up to the curb. Kerala rented a brand-new Vespa. Lucas straddled the seat, but Kerala pushed him back.

"I rented it and I'm driving," she said, throwing a leg over and sitting in front of Lucas. "You may have a map of Rome in your head, but I learned how to drive in Rome."

A Curukian in a black T-shirt gave Goper a set of keys, and the two gladiators crammed into a tiny Isetta microcar. Since Ekki couldn't fit in the passenger seat, he squatted in the back with his entire upper body sticking out of the sunroof.

Kerala cranked the gas on the Vespa. She drove so fast that Lucas nearly fell off the back. He clutched her waist as they zipped down the cobblestone streets. Kerala cut the moped hard right and rattled down via Milano, past scaffolding, and through a tunnel whose entrance was draped in vines. After ten minutes, Lucas told her to park outside a shoe store. They hopped off the Vespa and passed the shoe store doorway, which smelled of clean leather and air-conditioning.

Lucas thought about using the store as a diversion, but to his surprise, Goper and Ekki unfolded themselves from the tiny car behind them.

"I guess you know that we're almost at the Trevi Fountain," Kerala said.

"The plaza will be crowded," Lucas said.

"It's a perfect place to lose someone."

The fountain took up most of the piazza, and the rest of the space was jam-packed with tourists. Lucas could feel the crush of the crowd around them, but it felt safe and protected. He and Kerala tunneled through the throng. In the middle of the crowd Lucas got a good look at the famous fountain that he'd only seen online. The facade at the back stood some twenty meters high. At the center, a marble statue of Neptune, god of the sea, dominated the fountain. Water was flowing from underneath his shell-shaped chariot and down to the marble horses by the pool.

"Beautiful," Kerala said.

"It is."

Events that Lucas hadn't anticipated were unfolding in his favor. Tourists were clamoring to have their pictures taken with the pretend Roman gladiators. Lucas figured he would double down on his good luck. He took out two coins and gave one to Kerala. They tossed them over the crowd and into the fountain and made wishes.

The Good Company gladiators broke away from the tourists and separated. Goper went down the first street, and Ekki took the second. The Trevi Fountain was named for the intersection of three streets—*tre vie*.

Lucas and Kerala took the third.

"Let's go in here," Kerala said, pointing to a café. "It's hard to chase people who are not running."

The sweet smell of coffee and gelato covered

them like a sugar blanket. The place was packed and loud. Mostly tourists. A silenced TV showed the news with Italian subtitles. Lucas checked out the crowd and then did exactly what you're supposed to do in a gelato shop. He ordered something to eat. He got *stracciatella* and Kerala got *limone*. When they finally had their cups, they found a tiny marble table in the corner with only one chair remaining. Kerala gave Lucas her cup of gelato.

"I can feel my makeup running," she said. "I'll be right back."

Lucas sat and he took stock of his position. His eyes clicked back and forth from the open doorway to the TV. A few minutes later Kerala came through the noise of the café and back to the table. She was wearing no makeup, and she'd slicked her hair back with water. Lucas's mouth dropped. He couldn't believe how pretty she was. His inner gentleman kicked in, and he stood and gave her the chair.

"Wow," he said. "I've never seen you without makeup."

"It's horrible, isn't it?"

"Just the opposite," Lucas said.

"I'll take that as a compliment," she said with a huge smile.

"You know, you're weird," Lucas said.

"What do you mean?"

"Well," Lucas said. "You wear Goth makeup and clothes, and you know all these languages, but don't speak much. And then when you were speaking Italian with the passport guy, you seemed really happy."

"Funny that you noticed," she said. "I feel like I'm more myself when I'm speaking other languages. It's like I don't have makeup on—that I don't have to hide who I am."

"Well you did just show up one day at the Globe Hotel Luxembourg, and no one knew anything about you. And that's all anybody still knows. So . . . what is your story?"

Kerala took a bite of gelato and looked up at Lucas. "My mother was from Gothenburg, Sweden, and my dad was Russian, and they both worked in IT. They were expats and worked all over the world. I was born in Kerala, in India. Hence the name. And I grew up speaking Swedish and Russian at home. We had an Indian nanny and I learned Urdu—Hindustani—from her. I studied English and Chinese at school and learned Italian here in Rome. So speaking different languages feels like home to me."

"How did you get to Luxembourg?"

She paused, and her face became ashen. Then she blurted out, "My parents were murdered here in Rome."

"What?!"

"Yeah," she said. "Apparently my father found someone stealing computer data, and they didn't like what he knew. They killed him and my mom. The Roman police found me, and child services put me in an orphanage. I lasted like three months, and then I broke out on my own, finally making it up to the Globe Hotel Luxembourg, where Mr. Benes took me in."

"That's an awesome but really sad story," Lucas said. "You should talk more often."

They both got quiet and ate their gelatos. Lucas half watched the TV and half kept his eye out the door looking for Goper and Ekki.

"Uh-oh," Kerala said, reading the subtitles on the screen.

"What?"

"Apparently the Roman police really are looking for you," she said.

Lucas looked at the TV and saw his Interpol picture. "I always wanted to be on TV," he said.

"Ha-ha," Kerala said. "There are blockades all over town." Her eyebrows dipped. "I can't get caught here, Lucas. I just know the Roman police would love to question me about why I fled."

"If we can get to Vatican City," Lucas said, "then that's a whole nother country."

Lucas moved to the doorway and checked out the scene. Goper and Ekki were clomping down the street straight toward the café where Lucas was standing. Goper gritted his teeth and slapped his metal visor down.

Forget the gelato, Lucas thought, dropping the cup onto the floor.

He snatched the chair out from under Kerala. "How do you say sorry in Italian?" he asked.

"Mi dispiace," Kerala said.

She nodded to Lucas like she knew exactly what he was going to do. And she would help by creating the distraction.

She yelled out into the café like a bank robber, "Everybody get down!" She repeated it in Italian, Swedish, Russian, Chinese, and Urdu. Just in case.

The entire café, tourists and waiters alike, dropped to the ground.

Goper stood in the doorway and leaned his head inside.

Lucas rotated, swinging the chair above the people squatting in the café. The metal seat clocked Goper's helmet so loudly that it sounded like a church bell ringing. The force and trajectory of the chair was so great that the Good Company guard stumbled backward into the street. He fell into Ekki behind him, and both collapsed, clattering onto the cobblestones like two felled trees.

"Mi dispiace," Lucas said to the gladiators moaning in the street. Then he picked up his gelato cup and spoon and set them on the table.

Kerala and Lucas glanced at each other. They didn't speak. They ran. They bolted back to the Vespa and took off toward Vatican City.

A STORM BREWING

Ancient Romans were imaginative in building their great society. They used architecture and new construction techniques to create aqueducts, the Roman Forum, and of course, the Colosseum. They designed their roads to encourage people to come into the city center.

This network of streets also made for a perfect series of roadblocks that were now preventing Lucas and Kerala from getting out of the city. They were forced to go against the grain in a completely round-about way to get to the Vatican.

Kerala buzzed the Vespa past the Forum ruins and around the Colosseum where thousands of gladiators, warriors, and animals fought and died to provide entertainment for ancient Roman spectators.

They stopped at a bridge that would take them beyond the Tiber and into the Trastevere neighborhood. On the other side a blue Lamborghini with the word *Polizia* written on its side waited.

Kerala pulled the Vespa up onto the sidewalk under the plane trees. She and Lucas stared down at the collection of plastic bottles that bobbed on the dam in the river.

"We could take a boat," Kerala said.

"We have a boat to catch," Lucas said.

"What time is it?"

Lucas closed his eyes. "Six minutes after five."

"That policeman in the Lamborghini is looking at us."

Lucas knew they couldn't outrun the fastest car in the Roman police department. The GPS in his head recalibrated, calculating a new way through a narrow cobblestone maze.

"Right after this tram passes, cross the tracks and head up that way," he said, pointing.

A police siren screeched from some narrow lane, and Kerala steered the Vespa in the opposite direction. They motored through streets that were almost not big enough for one moped. They zigged and zagged their way past cafés and sidewalk restaurants and apartments with flowers in the windows. When they cut across the campo de' Fiori, Lucas told Kerala to stop at the statue in the center of the piazza.

"What's up?" Kerala asked as she kicked her legs out to balance the moped.

"Nobody's following us," Lucas said. "You lost them. And I just wanted to see this statue of Bruno."

"Why?"

"He's my favorite mathematician."

"Sorry, but I don't have a favorite mathematician,"

Kerala said. "Who does? And why this guy?"

"Giordano Bruno was a mathematician who was burned at the stake on this very spot."

"Why?"

"Because he was a freethinker," Lucas said.

"Like you."

"And my mother."

Kerala motored the Vespa around the city workers who were cleaning up the piazza from the farmers' market earlier that day. Seven minutes later they crossed the Tiber and drove past St. Peter's Square and the Vatican, where the pope's guards must not have known that Lucas was wanted by Interpol. They cut left, and four minutes later they arrived unnoticed at the Roma San Pietro train station.

They boarded the next train and arrived at the port of Civitavecchia an hour later.

Lucas looked to the west past Fort Michelangelo. It had been a beautiful day in Rome. Now out over the Mediterranean Sea dark clouds were gathering.

It was clear: A storm was brewing.

ALL ABOARD

Groups of Curukians working as stevedores on the docks scanned stacks of shipping containers.

Lucas watched them for a second as they seemed to verify every number they encountered. He hoped they were still looking for pi, the wrong number he had given Ms. Günerro at her hotel in Las Vegas.

Kerala moved through the maze of metal boxes. Lucas followed between the rows of giant containers. Some were red, others blue and gray. They passed an entire stack of yellow crates with Chinese lettering. They weaved in and out of the labyrinth until they saw a cargo ship with the name *Leviathan* written on the side.

On the dock below, Astrid and Travis stood in the doorway of a brand-new container. Solar panels on its roof soaked up the sun.

Lucas and Kerala made their way over to the container.

"The phi container," Lucas said, pointing at the *Leviathan*, "the one we're looking for, is on that ship right there."

"And," Astrid said, leading lead them into the new

container, "this lovely little bungalow will be our home away from home for the next twenty-four hours. So come on in and make yourselves comfortable!"

"Did you do a sweep for a tracking device?" Lucas asked.

"It's clean," Travis said.

The shipping container was a metal box with six flat rectangular sides that had been converted into a cabin straight out of summer camp. On one side, seven narrow bunks were built into the wall. At the far end of the room there was a small table with foldout seats. The container also had a stovetop, microwave, fridge, porta-potty, and shower. One-way windows allowed them to look out safely. Three stand-up air conditioners kept the place freezing cold, and solar panels on the roof provided nearly unlimited power.

Jackknife, Travis, Mac, and Alister were already stretched out on their bunks, and Kerala collapsed on the first available mattress. Within the hour, the gantry crane locked in on the New Resistance container and lifted it. The big metal box swung over and onto the ship. The drone-operated crane slipped the New Resistance container on top of the others like a giant Lego block, making it completely indistinguishable.

LIKE MOTHER LIKE SON

Siba Günerro stood on the balcony and watched the storm over the Mediterranean Sea block out the setting sun.

Over the top of her glittering glasses she eyed T, who was dabbing her face with more makeup. The women waited in silence as they listened to Charles Magnus, who again was on the phone managing a problem.

"What do you mean?" Magnus said into the phone. "You sort of lost them? You either lost them or you didn't. Which is it?"

Magnus pressed the phone to his ear.

"Let me get this straight," he said. "The New Resistance kids are now stowaways in a private shipping container on a ship called the *Leviathan*? Is that correct?"

He nodded a few times.

"I'll turn on the homing device as soon as they set sail."

There was a pause.

"We'll meet you there," he said.

Magnus hung up and faced T and Ms. Günerro.

Ms. Günerro asked, "Where are they headed?"

"Barcelona," Magnus said.

T said, "We can drive."

"How long is the drive?" Ms. Günerro asked.

"A little better than thirteen hours," Magnus said.

"Perfect," T said. "We'll drive up the Italian coast, cross southern France, and be in northern Spain for breakfast."

"That sounds nice," Ms. Günerro said. "But we're still missing too many opportunities. The man you hired to work the passport office at the Rome airport was a clown. And Magnus, your bus driver was obviously incompetent, and now it seems like your stevedores were unable to find container number two nine five one four one dash three."

"But—" Magnus said.

"While we cannot correct your past mistakes," Ms. Günerro said, "you must do better in the future!"

"I have some North African Curukians," Magnus said, "who are dying for a fight."

"As soon as this storm blows through, dispatch the boys and have them board the *Leviathan* in the early hours of tomorrow morning. Tell them to secure my container and lock up the New Resistance in their little private hideaway. In the meantime tell Goper and Ekki to get the car ready to take us to Barcelona."

"Will do," Magnus said. "But I'll have to get new drivers for us."

"Why?"

CHAPTER THIRTY-FIVE

"Goper has a bad headache."

"And Ekki?"

"He's stuck," Magnus said. "He can't get out of his gladiator suit."

"Very well then," Ms. Günerro said. "Get someone."

There was a lull as Ms. Günerro turned and faced the Vatican and the lights of Rome surrounding it.

"If I may add something," T said.

"Go ahead," Ms. Günerro said.

"Lucas Benes's mother was a freethinking trouble-maker and he's surely no different. Maybe this a case of 'like mother like son.'"

"What are you getting at?" Ms. Günerro asked.

"I know firsthand that his mother hated water, dark water, especially," T said. "And I wouldn't be surprised if the boy has a similar fear."

Magnus asked, "What are you suggesting?"

"I'm suggesting the obvious solution," T said.

Ms. Günerro said, "Magnus?"

"Yes?"

"Let the North African Curukians in on Lucas's weakness. As soon as our contact has identified the container, tell them to get rid of the Benes boy, permanently."

PHI

The container ship motored through the Tyrrhenian Sea west of Italy. As the night sky grew darker, thick clouds collided and blocked out any remaining twilight. It was going to be a stormy night.

An upper-level disturbance that had been brewing all evening hit the *Leviathan* at ten minutes before ten. The New Resistance kids had already been asleep when the rain started falling. Lucas's eyes popped open as he woke to what sounded like machine guns pelting their metal cabin.

The storm was fast and furious. Waves began to lift the bow and slam the ship down. Sheets of rain and bombs of thunder and lightning attacked the ship and its cargo, making a deafening noise inside the bunk room. The only thing louder than the squall was the groaning crunch of the metal containers as they slammed against one another.

The sea swells began to increase, and the waves grew larger and more powerful. Travis jumped out of his bed and hit the safety light, which cast a dull yellow across the room. Then a massive roller—a wave bigger than most—slammed into the ship, soaking the

Leviathan and half of its cargo in seawater. The stacks of containers rocked like toy blocks.

A giant clap of thunder exploded right overhead and briefly shorted out the electrical current. The cabin fell into complete darkness.

Kerala screamed, "We're all going to die!"

"Just hold on!" Astrid called out.

Within moments seven flashlights lit up, and their beams crisscrossed the room. As far as Lucas could tell, everyone was hugging a mattress and pillow. Mac's face was green like he was going to be sick.

Normally ships from Rome to Barcelona traveled a northern route. But whoever was guiding this drone vessel from elsewhere must have known the weather was bad. The ship turned and angled southward to avoid the storm. Instead of heading directly to Barcelona, it powered toward North Africa.

Seawater now blasted the side of the hull as walls of wind and rain continued to pummel the cargo. There came a series of unreal groaning sounds, followed by loud bursts. The storm was ripping some of the metal boxes to shreds, and their steel doors were crashing onto the ship's deck. Containers screeched as they tore away from the moorings that held them in place. Some of the cargo boxes on deck spun out of control and then crashed through the railing and slipped into the sea.

Soon the weather calmed, and the kids let go of their pillows and relaxed. Outside, the containers that had broken loose were still sliding and spinning around on the deck. Then, just as the rain seemed to be easing up, another massive wave hit and washed over the bow. Water flooded the deck, sweeping some of the loose containers directly into the Mediterranean.

For thirty minutes the storm tossed the ship around, and then, just as quickly as the tempest had come, it moved on, and the *Leviathan* continued toward Africa's northern shore.

A few minutes later Mac got up and got some water from the minifridge. He addressed the whole group. "Can we get on with this already?"

Lucas knew that the cargo his mother had sent out some twelve years earlier was on the ship with him. Unless of course it had just been tossed into the sea. But he had to agree with Mac. It was time.

"The moon should be out in a minute," Travis said. "Let's go find this famous container."

"More like infamous," Mac said. "I mean, Lucas's mother stole it."

"When you take something that belongs to you," Jackknife said, "it's not stealing."

"And," Travis said calmly, "if Ms. Günerro gets hold of this container, then the Good Company will be able to kidnap more and more children and sell them into slavery."

"You are all idiots," Mac said. "The Good Company is a giant company. They're not going away."

"Maybe not the company," Astrid said. "But if we

can show that Ms. Günerro and Bunguu are working together, then she might go to jail. In fact I can't wait to make this call."

Astrid grabbed her phone. "Wait," she said. "My cell phone's dead."

Mac reached under his pillow. "No service for me, either."

"Could be the storm," Travis said.

Lucas tapped the monitor on the wall and opened the doors.

A waning gibbous moon floated across the night sky. Lucas turned off his flashlight. The air was cool, and he guessed it was about twenty-two degrees Celsius, seventy-two Fahrenheit. The wind blew slightly, and there was a hint of salt taste to it.

A block of containers leaned against the wall across from them. Some columns were six cubes high, while other stacks had only two or three. Lucas jumped over the gap and onto the next container roof. The others followed. There he found a metal ledge that they used as a step. The storm had created odd-shaped formations of containers, creating canals and channels.

Lucas hopped over an edge and shimmied down between two boxes to the next level. His feet found a tiny lip at the corner of each container, and he straddled the space between them. They worked their way through this maze of metal, and in a few minutes came to the deck.

The front of the ship looked like a tornado had hit it.

The contents of the containers were scattered pell-mell. Several doors had blown off, and the cargo had spilled out onto the deck. There were clothes and shoes everywhere. A clump of lawn mowers and generators jammed together next to couches and tables and chairs. Colored plastic toys blanketed the area.

Lucas spun around and faced everyone. "Okay, guys," he said. "Let's find this container and see what it really has in it."

Mac huffed. "Who died and made you captain of this ship?"

Astrid picked up the argument. "Lucas's mother, his birth mother, started the demise of the Good Company twelve years ago." She pointed an index finger at Mac. "So I think the logical person here to lead us today is that mother's son."

"And," Jackknife added, "it's his grandfather's diamonds that are in the container."

"Unless of course it's missing," Travis said. "I mean, more than sixteen hundred containers are lost at sea every year."

"Okay, okay," Mac said. "Since you're the boss, then what exactly are we looking for?"

Travis said calmly, "The container is intermodal."

"What's that supposed to mean?" Mac asked.

"It means," Travis explained, "the container can be transferred easily from different modes of transportation, like from a ship to a train to a truck."

Mac said, "So what are you trying to say?"

"It should be a small container," Jackknife explained. "About twenty feet in length, about six meters."

"Half the size of the bunk room," Alister said.

"Let's think," Travis said. "If we off-load in Barcelona, then the container would be up front, wouldn't it?"

"Sounds reasonable," Kerala said.

Lucas asked, "What side do we dock on in Barcelona?"

"In that port this ship will dock on the . . ." Jackknife gestured toward the left-hand side of the ship. "We'll dock on the port side. Unless they make special provisions for drone ships."

"So," Lucas said, "we're looking for a twelve-year-old, twenty-foot container on the front-left side of the ship."

Kerala asked, "What's the number again?"

"TNRU three three zero eight one six dash one," Travis said.

Lucas said, "Let's spread out a little."

The moon cast a bright light across the deck where the kids muddled through the debris.

Lucas and Jackknife broke off from the group and skittered around a pool of glass marbles. They stopped at the first door and checked the numbers. HAMBURG SÜD VANU 105491-8.

Nope.

Their eyes flashed from the numbers on one container to the next. Lucas and Jackknife quickly got into a rhythm as they zigzagged back and forth, deeper and deeper into the canyon of metal boxes.

They traversed a whole section of canals and rounded a corner in the middle of the ship. There they met up with Mac, Alister, and Travis at a pile of twenty-foot containers that were stacked like logs on a campfire. The doors had been blown off, and the contents, mostly electrical machinery and equipment, had spilled out onto the deck.

Mac shuffled away by himself, kicking some deflated footballs into the sea. Alister rummaged through piles of electrical equipment and generators, and he picked up what looked like a gun.

"What's that?" Lucas asked.

"It's a plasma torch."

"Oh yeah," Travis said, touching a cart loaded with equipment. "That's used for welding."

Alister's eyes lit up, and his bow tie rose under his chin. "But a plasma gun is way better," he said. "I love this machine. It can slice and dice anything."

Just then a big wave knocked into the side of the boat, and ocean spray showered them. Lucas peered into the next container.

"I wouldn't get in there," Alister said. "These doors came off because the container couldn't handle the pressure. If it falls, you'll be crushed to death in a second. And I do not want to see that."

The metal support beams in the ceiling were slanting to the right. These old containers wouldn't hold long. The phi container must be close.

Jackknife walked past Lucas and stepped inside.

He kicked something. "Hey," he said. "There's camping stuff in here."

Lucas shone his flashlight into the container.

"Look at this!" Jackknife said. "There's all kinds of stuff in here."

The metal box made a groaning sound as the ship rocked across another big swell.

"Get out of there!" Astrid said as she and Kerala joined the boys.

Travis stepped into an opening that had been blasted in the side of the next container. He panned his flashlight across the space. "This is so cool! There're surfboards in here. And Windsurfers. A whole bunch of them. And kite boards too. This stuff is going to California—my home."

"It's not your birthday," Astrid said. "And we're not going surfing. Now get out!"

Travis and Jackknife crawled out, looking like they had just gotten in trouble.

Lucas kicked some clothes into a huge pile as they moved to the front of the ship.

Kerala pointed a flashlight on the next clump of old twenty-foot containers. This geometric pile of metal boxes looked as if the storm had been building something. The containers were stacked vertically and horizontally.

"It looks like Stonehenge," Alister remarked.

Mac snarled, "You mean the prehistoric monument in England? Hardly!"

Astrid said, "Good eye, Alister. It does look like Stonehenge."

Lucas pointed his beam of light, and they read the numbers on the doors. The first read CMA CGM CAPE TOWN | CMSU 810983-9. The next read APL NEW YORK 009 | APZU 532501-4. Lucas kept scanning the numbers with the flashlight, and then he stopped.

Hidden behind the Stonehenge group he spotted an old container, the oldest he had seen. It was leaning at a forty-five-degree angle against the others in the pile. The doors were facing down, and Lucas pointed the flashlight on the side wall. He cocked his head sideways.

There in the top right-hand corner was the symbol Φ.

"That's the letter phi," Lucas said.

He pointed the beam of light on the other side. At the top there was a number all by itself: TNRU 330816-1.

The same number of his birth chart.

"That's it," Lucas said. "We found it!"

THE SEA AT NIGHT

Earlier that evening, a group of small rubber boats, dinghies, had departed ports in North Africa.

One boat left from Tripoli, the capital of Libya, two from the Tunisian resort town of Hammamet, and a fourth from the dock in Algiers, the capital of Algeria.

Each boat contained four Curukians.

All four vessels were aimed at a tracking device located inside the New Resistance container.

Hours later, deep in the middle of the Mediterranean, they came together and waited for the cargo ship, the *Leviathan*.

UNBREAKABLE

Lucas crawled over a pile of clothes and under the Stonehenge stack of containers. He looked up at the two doors. Even if they could tip the phi container on its side, they would still have to deal with the locks.

"We just saw a ladder," Astrid said.

She and Nalini took off and in a few seconds came back with a long telescoping ladder. Mac helped them lean it against the phi container, and then everyone turned and looked at Alister.

Alister pocketed his lock-picking tools and climbed up.

"Uh-oh," he said.

"What is it?" Travis asked.

Alister shook his head. "Some of these latches are sealed with metal dowels that have to be cut off just to make the hinges work. Then some of these padlocks are made with iron-alloy shackles. But worse than that . . . all of the keyholes have been filled with liquid steel."

Astrid said, "That would explain why it's never been robbed."

"So what do we do now?" Mac asked.

"Well," Alister said, climbing down. "We're not getting in this container through the doors."

Lucas moved around the side, letting his hand trail along rough metal bumps. Rust spots dotted the walls of the metal box. Years of sea salt caked the rim.

Lucas ducked underneath. In the floor he spotted a tiny hole about the size of a little finger.

"There's a hole in it," Jackknife called out as he crawled under with Lucas.

The others gathered. Lucas beamed light into the hole while Jackknife and Alister squatted next to him.

Astrid asked, "Did someone drill the hole?"

"No," Jackknife said. "It's rusted."

Mac knelt underneath and started banging on the bottom of the container. A few seconds later Kerala noticed something and put a light on it.

"Look," she said picking it up. "A diamond!" She rolled it between her thumb and index finger. "Now, this is beautiful."

Everyone moved in closer and marveled at it.

"That could be a Kapriss diamond," Travis said.

Mac said, "And Ms. Günerro's coming to get it."

"How do you know?" Astrid said.

"You think she's just going to let this go?" Mac asked. "She loves diamonds and ivory, and there are elephant tusks in there. Right?"

"If there is ivory in there," Astrid said, "then it'll be turned over to Interpol, and they'll destroy it all."

"That's a waste!" Mac said. "You don't want the elephants to have died for no reason."

"You don't get it," Astrid said. "If you destroy the supply of ivory tusks, then people can't buy it. If they stop buying, then the poachers will stop killing elephants."

"Rich people like Ms. Günerro always get what they want," Mac said. "That's why I want to be rich."

"Like Ms. Günerro?" Travis asked.

"Why not!" Mac said.

The *Leviathan* turned west and slowed its speed. The storm had passed, but from this direction the wind was stronger and more humid. A little chilly. The swells were much bigger, and more spray came over the sides.

A clump of lingering clouds floated across the sky and dimmed the moonlight. Lucas and Alister crawled out from under the metal box and stepped back several feet to study the arrangement of containers.

It did look like Stonehenge.

Lucas glanced at Alister. His father and Lucas's mother had plotted to stop the Good Company. For a dozen years they had at least kept the pressure on Siba Günerro and slowed her down.

Alister went back to the container and jabbed his fingers into the rust that ran across the bottom.

He grinned at Lucas and gave him a quick knuckle punch, and they returned their attention to the others.

"Let's get back to the bunk room," Lucas said.

"Yeah," Astrid said. "We found what we were looking for, and as soon as my phone starts working again, we'll call it in."

Back at the bunk room they sat around Kerala's and Astrid's beds and played cards. Lucas tried, but he couldn't concentrate. He was still too distracted by the container they had found.

He wondered if he would learn more about who he was if he knew who his grandfather had been.

At that moment Lucas felt like a sardine crammed into a metal tin. He lost his third hand in a row and decided to make a change.

"I'm sleeping outside tonight," Lucas announced to the group.

Before anyone could say anything, Lucas tossed his cards on the bed and unlatched the door. He scrambled down a canal to a container filled with dry sleeping bags and camping pillows. In a few minutes he was back at the bunk room. There he climbed on top of the container and laid out his sleeping bag next to the solar panels.

Lucas breathed in the night air and let out a sigh. It was over. He had found what he had come for and connected with his mother and his grandfather. In his mind he spoke to them.

He stared up at the starry Mediterranean sky and listened to the hum of the engines rumbling away. The *Leviathan* lowered its speed again, and Lucas felt like he could finally relax.

Or so he thought.

CAMPING OUT

The sea that night was dark and had finally calmed down, and the sky was full of stars.

It isn't so bad, Lucas thought, *to be this far out in the middle of nowhere, all alone.*

The Mediterranean Sea was for a long time the intersection of the known earth. *Medius* means "middle" and *terra* means "earth." The area was the center of trade, with goods and produce shipped back and forth from the Middle East to the Atlantic Ocean and all points between.

Some of the greatest civilizations the world has ever known bordered this wide expanse of water— Rome, Egypt, the Ottoman Empire, Greece.

There was history here.

Lucas's family history was here too. The lights of the African cities to the south and the sparkling stars in the sky . . . his mother's secret messages . . . his grandfather's precious diamonds.

A long time ago the southern part of the Mediterranean Sea harbored some of the world's most notorious pirates. The Barbary Coast was at one time populated with "barbaric" bandits. The US Marine Corps fought its first land battle on foreign soil there in response to pirate raids.

Lucas's thoughts returned to his family. His mother had set this whole plan in motion a dozen years earlier. A hotel cleaning lady had beaten Ms. Siba Günerro, the Good Company, and the Bunguu family at their own game. Lucas's mother and grandfather might actually be the ones who had the last laugh.

Lucas curled his sleeping bag up around his neck and got comfortable for the night. The rumble of the ship's slow engines churning through the water lulled him to the edge of sleep.

As the *Leviathan* motored into the full Mediterranean Sea, she cut through the waters between the Italian island of Sardinia and the continent of Africa.

Centuries before, the Phoenicians were the great sailors of this region.

When they sailed afar, they stopped in Carthage, in what is now Tunis, the capital of Tunisia, where the Afri people lived. Sailors called this dusty part of the Sahara "Afar," which later may have given us the name for the entire African continent.

Regardless of how it was named, Africa was still a land afar.

Unfortunately for Lucas, as he dropped into sleep, Africa was not far enough away.

CLINK. CLINK. CLINK.

Lucas woke up, his eyes wide in the dark night.

His internal fear factor raised the thin hairs on the back of his neck. He and the cargo ship had sailed into international waters, a place where anything could happen. It was a dangerous spot. And he could feel it all over.

Lucas held his breath and waited for proof.

His first concrete clue was the distinct sound of a compressed-air cannon firing.

Pthtt.

Lucas sat up in his perch on top of the container.

At the front of the ship a metal grappling hook flew over the railing. It sailed through the night and passed through the ship's light beams. Lucas spotted the distinctive teeth on the hook as it grabbed hold of the handrails.

Clink.

Metal on metal.

Someone was below.

In the water.

About to climb up.

Then from the bow and the sides he saw three

more hooks flying over the railing.
Clink. Clink. Clink.
It wasn't someone.
It was an invasion.

ROUGH SEAS

Lucas stared at the grappling hooks that clung to the railing, and his eyes followed the attached ropes to where they fell over the ship's edge and down toward the sea.

It was quiet for a second until he saw the ropes tighten, and he heard the murmur of a motorized winch.

Four of them buzzing in the night.

Lucas had used a similar-sounding winch back at the hotel in Las Vegas. A simple press of a button, and the motor could pull a grown man straight up the line at nine meters a minute.

Lucas peeled himself out of the sleeping bag and slid down the side of the container. The air was humid and chilly. He straddled a gap and swung down to the next level, climbing around to the front of the sleeping compartment where the others were. Hoping to wake his friends, he lightly tapped on the walls with his fingernails. He slowly opened the door. When there was space enough, Lucas poked his head inside.

"Psst," he said into the dimly lit room.

"What?" Astrid asked. "We have to sleep. Tomorrow's

a big day."

"Curukians," Lucas announced in a whisper. "At least four of them are boarding the ship right now."

Travis pointed his flashlight at Lucas in the doorway.

"Behind you!" Jackknife said, suddenly awake.

Lucas didn't see the boy, but he heard him. He grabbed hold of the doorframe and donkey-kicked backward. He hit the boy square in the gut, and the kid didn't move. Lucas spun and jumped down to the next container and came face-to-face with another Curukian. This was a big kid, and Lucas knew he couldn't take him.

Fortunately, Jackknife had his back.

The Brazilian came flying across the top of the roof. Lucas heard him and leaned out of the way as Jackknife cut through the air. His feet jammed straight down on the boy's collarbones. Lucas heard the crack. The Curukian clutched his clavicles and crumbled into a ball.

Travis and Alister scrambled out of the sleeping compartment, shining flashlights on the scene.

Curukians were swarming.

Mac came out of the bunk room and took the black stone necklace out of his shirt. He held it up in the air. "We're up here!" he yelled out into the night.

They all turned and glared at Mac.

In a way Lucas felt like he couldn't believe what Mac had just done, but in another way he had always known something was not right.

Astrid said, "You really are a traitor!"

"I knew it," Jackknife said.

"You bunch of do-gooders," Mac said. "Me and my buddies are going to take some of these diamonds and live like kings."

On the deck below they could hear several more Curukians scrambling up the containers.

"Well, Mac," Astrid said. "I don't care how rich you want to be. But having people or animals die or get killed just so that you can get rich is never worth it."

"Think whatever you want," Mac said. "My aunt says she doesn't care how many elephants die or how many kids are kidnapped for us to be rich. So I'm here to get money any way I can."

"Who's your aunt?" Travis asked.

"Siba Günerro."

Jackknife looked like he was ready to kill Mac. "You were in on this the whole time!"

"Yeah," Mac said. "Good Company computers can hack into just about anything—especially New Resistance software."

Astrid asked, "But how did your Curukian friends find us tonight out here on the ship?"

Mac tapped his necklace. "Wearable GPS."

Jackknife said, "You know we're not giving up without a fight."

Mac smiled. "Suit yourself."

There was a painfully quiet pause, then Curukians

wearing wet-suit shorts and rash guards started climbing up the containers and closing in on them. Scuba knives were strapped to their calves.

"Astrid!" Travis called out. "Watch it!"

Mac did a standing back flip and nailed Travis in the chest, knocking him down.

Astrid and Kerala spun around. Both girls jumped down one level and faced off with two more Curukians. They fought side by side, punching and kicking the boys, pushing them to the back of the container. The two Curukians stumbled to the edge. Kerala nudged them both just a little and they fell to the next container, which had been knocked slanted by the storm. From there the boys slid down into a hole that had no obvious exit.

Lucas felt the air moving by his ear. He ducked as a Curukian's enormous arm swung over his head. With Lucas still squatting, Jackknife leapfrogged over Lucas's shoulders and sprang into the air. His body twisted, and his right heel connected with the kid's rib cage. The force threw the boy backward, and he stumbled to the end of the container, nearly falling off. He regained his balance, stooped, and extended his hand over the edge. Another Curukian grabbed hold of his arm and began climbing up. Lucas thought about stepping on the boy's fingers, but then he heard Kerala scream.

"Lucas! Jackknife!"

Threatening with scuba knives, four Curukians

shoved the others—Kerala, Astrid, Travis, and Alister—into the bunk room. One of the boys slammed the door and slapped a new padlock on it and tossed Mac the key.

Everything was happening too fast.

Another Curukian crawled up onto the container. Lucas guessed he weighed at least one hundred kilos—more than two hundred and twenty pounds. Jackknife moved in. With his forearm he struck the Curukian in the Adam's apple just as he was standing up. The kid didn't flinch. He rubbed his hand across his throat like he was wiping it with a napkin.

Lucas ridge-punched the big guy in the temple, but the Curukian simply scratched his head and kept moving.

The only tool left for Lucas was his brain. He needed to think.

On the deck there were plenty of actual tools that they could use to defend themselves. He motioned to Jackknife, and the boys jumped to the roof of the next container and began their descent. They scrambled between the metal boxes, cutting left and right. They could hear the rumble of the Curukians climbing down after them. Lucas and Jackknife moved faster, and in a matter of seconds they dropped five floors to the ship's deck.

Jackknife panted, "How many are down so far?"

"I think four, maybe."

"These guys are huge."

Jackknife and Lucas started rummaging through the debris scattered on the deck, looking for something they could use as a weapon.

That's when Lucas noticed the ship was barely moving. Whoever was piloting this drone ship must have slowed it down so the Curukians could board.

Jackknife said, "How many do you think they brought?"

"Four boats of four," Mac said as he hopped down from a container and onto the deck. "Plus me—that makes nineteen."

Lucas and Jackknife exchanged puzzled looks. Lucas figured Mac was trying to make his group seem bigger. Neither boy corrected Mac's math.

Four giant Curukians emerged from behind Mac and stood with their arms crossed over their chests. In the moonlight Lucas got a better look at them. They were barefoot and bearded. But mostly they were huge.

Names like Goliath and Sasquatch came to Lucas's mind. He thought, *How come some kids are giants, while others, the same age, are puny?*

It was true. You could be born on the same exact day as someone else, and by the time you hit ten or eleven or twelve, a girl your age could look like a movie star and you could still look like a first grader.

Another giant approached Lucas and Jackknife and towered over them. He wore a black eye patch over his right eye.

"Mac?" Eye Patch asked. "You know which container it is?"

"Yep."

Eye Patch pointed at Lucas. "Good. We have specific instructions for the Benes boy."

Jackknife looked like he was about to bicycle-kick these kids. Then he let out a grunt. Four new Curukians had just tackled him from behind and laid him out on the deck.

"Put him with the others," Mac ordered, giving them the key.

While they carted Jackknife away, Eye Patch squeezed Lucas around the chest and kneed him in the back, lifting him in the air. Lucas tried to kick free, but two more Curukians quickly grabbed his feet.

"Bring him over this way," Mac said.

The three boys carried Lucas and shuffled him across the deck to the opening in the railing that had been blasted off during the storm.

Lucas looked up and saw Jackknife watching.

Clutching his wrists and ankles, the Curukians started swinging Lucas like a human hammock.

Maybe this is just a game, Lucas thought. *They aren't really going to . . .*

Mac counted as Lucas tried to wiggle out. They had him in a death grip.

"One," Mac said as Lucas's body swung up to where the railing used to be.

Lucas's butt soared toward the moon. "Two."

They swung him back, and Mac drumrolled on Lucas's belly. He called out, "Three!"

Lucas went out over the edge of the ship, sailing into the night sky. Flying solo. He flailed his arms and tried to fly back to the boys who had just thrown him off. But this was no cartoon. A body in motion will not stop until acted upon by an external force. The next thing that would stop his fall would be the water.

Lucas dropped. He was either going to land a back breaker or a belly buster. If he stood any chance of survival, he had to change course. He righted himself and knifed into the water. It wasn't a pretty dive, but he managed to get his hands in front of him and save his back and belly.

But the angle sent him deeper into his greatest fear. Dark water.

Underwater, Lucas opened his eyes. He saw nothing but blackness. The fall from the ship's deck had sent him down deep. He felt like a missile descending into the water. His ears tightened, and with a last bit of hope, he arched his body and aimed back toward the ship.

He swam as hard as he could, trying to pull himself out. But it seemed to be taking forever.

Since he couldn't see, he thought he might actually be swimming down, farther away from the air that his lungs were desperately in need of. Above his head the ship's engines murmured. It was to his left. His ears were loosening. He pushed and sprang out of the water and bobbed on the surface of the sea.

The ship he had just been thrown off was about halfway past him. Even if he could swim to the hull, he wouldn't be able to hold on to anything. The best he could hope for was to be sliced by the keel or chewed up by the propeller. At least he would die quickly, he thought. But he was even too far away for that to happen.

The cold reality hit him. He was in the middle of the Mediterranean Sea at night. Alone. In dark water. About to drown.

CHAPTER 42

SURVIVAL OF THE MOST ADAPTABLE

The dark always muddied Lucas's thinking.

He couldn't tell if he was in a nighttime cerebral vision or if he was really drowning. Self-doubt flooded his heart, and a voice in his head told him it was already over. He had failed, and he should give in and die.

Lucas pushed the thoughts back. He reached out of the water and gulped in a huge breath. He opened his mouth as wide as it would go and filled his lungs with air.

He knew what was happening. He was not dreaming. He was drowning.

His head sank again below the surface of the water. He couldn't see what he needed to do. But the unknown and the unexpected were the very things that made Lucas calculate the hardest and took him the furthest. This time he would have to dig even deeper.

Everything the woman with long black hair had told him came to mind.

He had been in dark water before—in Tierra del Fuego when his adoptive mother had saved him. This time there was no mother to save him. No New Resistance. No ice chest. There was only Lucas.

Then he heard his own voice. "Never give up. Never. Ever."

Determination coursed through his veins.

Lucas lurched up and inhaled again, and on this breath seawater filled his nose. The salt burned his nostrils, and the water shocked his whole system like he had been electrocuted. He coughed and started treading water.

Just as Lucas's lungs were filling with air, one of the boats that the Curukians had used to board the cargo ship hit him in the head. The rubber dinghy rode over Lucas and shoved him underwater. They had left it attached to the *Leviathan*.

He wasn't out of trouble yet, but he wasn't dead, either.

If he could get on the dinghy, he could at least float with the *Leviathan* to Barcelona. He wouldn't have to drown.

Lucas went back down, and the dinghy passed over him. Alone again. Had he missed his chance?

He stabbed at the water and chased after the little boat. He swam harder than he had ever swum in his whole life. Kick paddle paddle. In those few moments Lucas was sure he was setting an Olympic record in freestyle. Arm stroke after arm stroke. He focused on his kicking, knowing that it would propel him through the water faster and straighter.

He was still maybe two meters behind the dinghy. He was only keeping up. He wasn't gaining. And he knew he couldn't maintain the pace for long. He pushed harder and dug deeper, his hands cupped for maximum propulsion.

His left hand hit something. His finger just grazed it. It was fuzzy and long like a snake. He flutter-kicked super fast, and his hand touched the object again. It was a rope dragging in the water, and it was attached to the little boat.

With both hands he clawed at the rope. He had it. But it was slipping. Lucas swirled the rope and hitched it around his left forearm. He turned over and hoped it would hold.

The rope tightened around his arm and dragged him through the sea. The water coned over his head, creating a cocoon where he forgot about the darkness around him. But Lucas knew he couldn't stay in this position long.

Lucas spun and shimmied up the rope to the back of the dinghy. With his last joule of energy, he flung himself over the side and into the boat and crawled to the bow. Wet and cold, he huddled there among a nest of climbing ropes, wishing for something to drink and shivering from exhaustion.

He closed his eyes, and somewhere in the early hours of the new day, sleep came to him.

CHAPTER 43

IF YOU CAN'T BEAT 'EM

Lucas felt the light and the heat.

He flung the blanket of ropes off him and looked out from the little boat. He had no idea where he was. The sun was low in the western sky, and the *Leviathan* was churning northward, dragging him and the dinghy along.

The sun is setting? he thought. *I slept all day?*

Lucas sat up and tried to get his bearings.

He kept watch for at least an hour, and then to the northwest, a land mass appeared. Lucas rubbed his eyes. The coastline was dotted with powerboats and sailboats zipping across the water. He figured they were about two and a half kilometers, about one and a half miles, offshore. Soon a ferryboat passed nearby with the name *Islas Baleares* written on the side. They were in the Spanish waters near Mallorca.

At the speed the *Leviathan* was traveling, they wouldn't make Barcelona until the next morning. Lucas knew he couldn't spend another night in the dinghy by himself, with no food or drink. He needed to make a move.

Hoping to find something for his thirst, he opened

a small stow box that was located under the seat. There were no drinks, but he did find a treasure trove of other useful items.

First there was a compressed-air cannon the Curukians had used to board the ship. Next Lucas found a harness and a motorized winch. At the bottom of the box he found a set of titanium scuba knives and a wet suit.

An idea blossomed.

Lucas's hair and clothes were damp and crusted with salt from his swim earlier that morning. He quickly changed into the wet-suit shorts and shirt and slipped on the climbing harness. With a neoprene wrap he strapped a diver's knife to his calf. Then he coiled the ropes he had slept in and looped them over his shoulder.

With the press of a button the winch pulled him up from the dinghy to the ship's deck. It took about three minutes to cover the distance.

In a way, having been thrown overboard helped his situation. He had been gone for almost a full day, and everyone would think that he was dead.

With the sun setting behind him, Lucas hurdled the railing and landed on the deck, where his bare feet squeaked. From somewhere on the other side of the containers he could hear voices.

Lucas moved along the perimeter. He threaded himself through the maze of metal boxes and took up a position close to the front of the ship. There he squatted behind a container door that was swinging on one broken hinge. He peered through the crack between the door and the container.

The Curukians had clearly taken over, with Mac in charge. At the front of this open area Mac had managed to create a makeshift office with a desk, chair, and couch. He was leaning back in his seat, pretending to smoke a cigar.

In a matter of one day each boy had staked out a section of the deck for the stuff he presumably wanted to steal. It looked like a small flea market.

A tall, lanky boy was collecting video-game controllers. He had tucked himself under a sheet of plywood, where he was hunched over, jamming on the joysticks that weren't connected to any screen.

Next to him there was a thin kid who had raided a candy container and was organizing everything by color.

One boy collected phones; another rounded up rubber duckies. As far as Lucas could see, everyone had tons of food and drinks.

Some of the boys seemed to be working for another purpose.

A few were collecting hooks, pulleys, and thick cables. Probably getting ready to hoist the container away, Lucas figured. Another Curukian was caring for four of the boys who were lying on cots in what was presumably the infirmary.

Eye Patch and another kid had set up a giant television

powered by a noisy generator. They looked like they were getting ready for a sleepover.

Someone turned on the TV, and the boys settled in to their areas.

Lucas knew there was no way for him to take on so many Curukians, even under the cover of darkness. These giant Curukians had already locked his friends in the bunk room and had thrown him overboard.

This was now officially a case of "if you can't beat 'em, join 'em."

The generator powering the television was louder than the sound coming from the TV. But the boys were glued to it. For Lucas it would provide a perfect distraction all night.

Nearby a boy in a black baseball cap leaned against a container, collecting marbles. Lucas had found his victim. He scrambled back to where he and Jackknife had seen a pool of marbles earlier. He picked up a few and returned to his spot.

Squatting just behind the swinging container door, Lucas launched three marbles at the boy in the black cap. The little glass balls rolled across the deck and hit his leg. The boy swatted at them and grabbed two. The third marble rolled back toward Lucas.

The boy got up and chased after it like a cat chasing a string.

He rounded the corner where Lucas was hiding, and just as the kid looked up, Lucas flung the door closed and slammed him in the head. The boy stumbled and moaned a little before passing out. In one motion Lucas stole his baseball cap and dragged the kid to midship, where one of the boats was tied up.

Lucas looped a rope harness around the boy and lowered him through the railing and down onto the paddles in the boat below. Using his scuba knife, Lucas cut the rope holding the boat and set it adrift. The tide would soon wash it ashore.

Then Lucas scurried back to the front deck and took the boy's place. Carefully keeping his head down, he ate and drank and watched TV all night long with his new best friends.

A FRENCH CONNECTION

Just past sunrise the next day Lucas woke to a throbbing sound.

He squinted and spotted a small helicopter, a Robinson R22, flying over the water toward them. Lucas stayed still and watched. Some of the other boys got up and waved. A second later Lucas read the name on the helicopter's side door. *Interpol.*

There wasn't much time left to make something happen. The *Leviathan* swayed in the water with the Barcelona harbor just off to the northwest. Whoever was piloting the drone ship was stopping it before they docked in the marina.

The *Leviathan*'s automatic chains clanged through their hawseholes, and the anchors splashed into the sea, bringing the cargo ship to a full and complete stop. For a second the Interpol helicopter hovered over the bow.

Lucas glanced at his clothes. No one had noticed him all night. He was dressed like the Curukians in wet-suit shorts and shirt with a diver's knife strapped to his calf. He pulled the brim of his black cap down over his eyes and joined the Curukians.

CHAPTER FORTY-FOUR

The R22 was tiny and took up little space as it landed on the deck.

The helicopter door opened, and a woman wearing an Interpol uniform and long black boots stepped out. Her name tag read AGENT CHARLOTTE JANSSENS. She took off her headset and tossed it back onto her seat. Following this officer was a boy Lucas immediately thought he recognized. The kid carried a cane and looked exactly like Hervé, the French guy who kept showing up everywhere when they were in Paris.

Couldn't be, Lucas thought.

Acting like the boss, Mac stood and shook hands with them. They spoke for a second, and then Lucas heard the French kid say to Mac, "But of course!"

It was most definitely Hervé Piveyfinaus.

This could be really good news, Lucas thought. *Or really bad.*

EXPECT THE UNEXPECTED

Lucas positioned himself at the back of a clump of Curukians and watched.

Wind swirled from the helicopter with deep, thumping throbs as the engine came to a rest. Lucas felt like his heart was beating louder than the spinning blades.

Mac led Hervé and the Interpol agent down a series of steps to his makeshift office. He motioned for them to sit on the couch.

Hervé set his cane down and sank into the cushions, but the officer stood and surveyed the ship's deck.

She spoke over the sound of the TV generator. "I'm Agent Charlotte Janssens with Interpol," she said. "What are you boys doing on this ship?"

Mac sat up in his chair and surveyed his crew. "We work for Ms. Günerro and the Good Company," he said. Then he pointed toward the couch. "Just like Hervé here."

Hervé sat up, his French accent thick. "How do you know me?"

"I've studied your file," Mac said. "You're supposedly

trying to leave the Good Company and help the New Resistance, but you can't seem to get away because you know the Good Company does everything good."

"Not true!"

"So why are you here?" Mac asked.

"Ms. Günerro," Hervé said, "ordered me to be here."

"That's because she doesn't trust you," Mac said.

Agent Janssens stepped forward. "I'm looking for Lucas Benes."

Mac leaned back and cupped his hands behind his head. "Lucas went overboard," he said. "Literally."

Hiding his face under the brim of the cap, Lucas looked around at the other boys. None of them recognized him. Still, he was afraid that the nervous pounding of his heart would give him away.

Eye Patch stood next to Mac and grinned. "Arr," he said, sounding like a pirate. "Lucas went off after a whale!"

The other Curukians suddenly burst out laughing like a pack of hyenas. Lucas played along.

Agent Janssens wiped the sweat from her brow. "You mean to tell me," she said, "that Lucas Benes jumped ship?"

"Not in that way," said the big kid who had helped throw Lucas off. "You know, maybe Lucas wanted to go for a swim or maybe he took one of the lifeboats. It's a free world, you know. He's probably on one of the beaches back there at Mallorca having a fruit drink and working on his tan."

"Where are the others?" Hervé said.

"There are no others," Mac said. He gestured toward Lucas and the Curukians on the deck. "It's just us."

Hervé grabbed his cane and shook it at the Interpol agent. To Lucas this was a good sign.

Agent Janssens's eyebrows crinkled as she stared at a pile of diamonds on Mac's desk.

"You're not allowed to take anything off this ship, you know," she said.

"Yeah we know," Mac said.

"I'm also looking for a container," Agent Janssens said.

"Well," Mac said, extending his hand, "you've come to the right place."

The Curukians laughed.

"I'm looking for a particular container," she said.

"We've already located it for you," Mac said. He pointed toward the Stonehenge clump of containers. "It's right over there behind that pile."

"Good," Agent Janssens said. "In just a minute Ms. Günerro is coming with a heavy-lift helicopter to remove the container from this ship."

What! Lucas thought. *In a minute?* He looked out over the water and spotted a giant helicopter motoring toward them.

They were coming to get the phi container.

Mac stood. "Ms. Günerro doesn't like to wait," he said, signaling the boys with the hooks and pulleys and straps. "We better get things ready before she gets here."

This group of boys went behind the Stonehenge pile and began hooking the straps to the phi container, preparing it to be lifted off the ship. While these boys worked, Agent Janssens and Hervé walked around the deck inspecting the cargo that was scattered everywhere.

They stopped right next to Lucas.

Cold reality hit Lucas. In a few minutes Ms. Günerro was going to take the Kapriss diamonds away by helicopter. This time forever.

Do I just let her take the container? Lucas's thoughts ran negative. *Or do I try to trick her into taking a different one? Then I would take the diamonds and give them to . . . to charity? What would I do with diamonds?* Lucas remembered that with the Good Company he needed to think backward. *It's not what a person would do with diamonds. The question is what would someone* not *do with diamonds?*

His idea formed. Lucas would do something entirely unexpected.

WORK AS A TEAM

Lucas could see the boys on top of the Stonehenge pile connecting several thick cables to the phi container. He turned and faced Hervé's profile and nudged the cane with his foot.

The French kid cut Lucas a glance.

Hervé's eyes connected with Lucas's, and they lit up. "Lucas!" Hervé said.

Lucas turned his back and Hervé stopped himself, and his tone calmed as he spoke to Agent Janssens. "Lucas Benes," he said, "would never have been on this ship without the New Resistance. They work as a team."

Agent Janssens's eyebrows dipped. "So where are they, then?"

Hervé scanned the mountain of metal boxes. "The New Resistance often travels in containers," Hervé said. "And I recently heard that they are now solar powered. So they would have to be up top." He pointed with the cane. "Like that one there."

Agent Janssens marched straight up to Mac. "I may have a special arrangement with Mr. Magnus, Ms. Günerro, and the Good Company," she said. "But I don't take kindly to children lying to police officers. Give me the key."

Mac dug a reluctant hand in his pocket and pulled out a key ring and handed it to Agent Janssens, who took off climbing up the stacks of containers.

A second later Lucas and Hervé left the main deck and hid behind another broken door. Within minutes Agent Janssens was leading the group of New Resistance kids back down to the deck.

"Psst," Lucas called from behind the door.

"Lucas?" Jackknife said.

Hervé and the New Resistance kids stopped and huddled behind the door with Lucas while Agent Janssens continued down to the front of the ship.

"I thought you were dead," Kerala said.

"Never," Lucas said.

Hervé put a big smile on and waved down to Agent Janssens and Mac and the other Curukians.

"Hervé?" Astrid asked. "What are you doing here?"

The French kid put his head back behind the door. "I'm here to help."

"You always show up everywhere," Travis said.

"But of course."

Astrid turned to Lucas. "Jackknife said they threw you overboard."

"They did," he said. "Long story, but I climbed back up."

Travis pointed toward the giant helicopter that was now approaching the ship.

Jackknife said, "Let me take a wild guess who this is coming to our party."

Lucas said, "She's here to take the container."

"We can't let that happen," Alister said.

"We must," Hervé said, "make it impossible."

"I need a minute," Lucas said. "And some of Alister's know-how with that plasma torch."

Astrid nodded. "I can stall Ms. Günerro for five, ten minutes," she said.

Lucas motioned for Alister to come on.

Alister stopped. "The plasma torch and generator are going to be clunky," he said. "We'll need help."

Jackknife spoke up. "Astrid and Travis are the best with arguments," he said. "Kerala and I can back you up."

"Kerala," Alister said, "get the liter of gas from the bunk room and meet us at the phi container behind Stonehenge."

Lucas said to Astrid, "Just make sure everyone still thinks I'm lost at sea."

"Good luck," Astrid said.

"Thanks," Lucas said. "I'll need it."

ENTER MS. GÜNERRO

The Chinook helicopter with its two rotor blades hovered over the open space on the deck. The side door slid open, and Charles Magnus stood in the doorway. He was wearing gray-and-white-camouflaged fatigues and goggles. The head of Good Company Security unfurled two ropes down to the deck of the *Leviathan*.

Behind him, Ms. Günerro, wearing blue-and-white-camouflaged fatigues, appeared.

Looking like synchronized acrobats in the Cirque du Soleil, Magnus and Ms. Günerro descended their ropes and waved to the Curukians below. Their boots sparkled, and the loose fabric on their outfits flapped in the wind. The boys on deck formed a circle, and Magnus and Ms. Günerro dropped into the middle of them.

As soon as her feet hit the deck, Ms. Günerro asked, "Where are my diamonds?"

THE OPPOSITE OF THE OPPOSITE

With a pair of cat-eye goggles stretched across her eyes, Siba Günerro looked out over the deck of the cargo ship. The president and CEO of the Good Company gripped the railing as the *Leviathan* rocked in the warm water off the eastern coast of Spain.

The sunlight sparkled on the sea, highlighting the yachts and fishing vessels, the ferries and cruise ships that were moving to and from the old harbor. Due west, the skyline of Barcelona burned in the August haze.

Thundering overhead, the giant Chinook heavy-lift helicopter hovered in anticipation.

Ms. Günerro removed her goggles and flung them to Magnus, who was standing just behind her. She slipped on a pair of cat-eye sunglasses and inspected the debris scattered across the deck. From a pouch on her outfit she pulled a satchel of frozen peas and popped one in her mouth.

She strutted over to Mac's "office."

"Well, well, well," she said. "It certainly looks like my ship has finally come in."

Talking over the sound of the helicopter and TV

generator, Ms. Günerro gave a speech to the Curukians who were gathered in front of her. They clapped wildly at everything she said.

Still dressed as a Curukian scuba diver, Lucas led Alister and Jackknife as they zipped around the middle section of the ship and located the welding cart, the plasma torch, and its generator. They carried the equipment down through the gaps between the giant boxes and set up shop behind the Stonehenge of containers.

Lucas scurried up the ladder and checked on the hoisting cables the Curukians had placed on top of the phi container. He halfway unlocked two of them so that it looked like they were still attached.

When he climbed back down to the deck, Kerala was already filling the welding equipment tank with gas. Jackknife hooked up the generator while Alister attached the air and power supply hoses to the plasma torch.

Alister screwed in the pilot igniter and adjusted the air pressure and amperage. Then he suited up with a welder's helmet and gloves. He gave them a double thumbs-up, then positioned himself about halfway down the side of the phi container where he found a soft spot in the metal.

Alister flipped open his visor. "Let it rip," he said, and slapped the face mask closed.

Jackknife fired up the machines.

Alister clicked his gun, and a short blue flame jumped out. He knelt and put the torch to the bottom of the container and slowly began cutting into it. As soon as he touched the plasma gun to the metal, white sparks shot out.

"Curukians," Kerala said. "Three o'clock."

There were two boys who looked like they were on security detail pacing the perimeter of the ship.

Lucas gave Kerala his diving knife. "Drop those guys in one of the boats," he said.

Without saying a word, Jackknife and Kerala chased the boys down and jumped them from behind. While his friends dealt with the Curukians, Lucas crawled under the Stonehenge containers. There he burrowed himself deep inside a mound of clothes. He moved to the edge of the pile and peered out. From this point of view Lucas could see the main deck. He couldn't quite hear everything. The TV generator and the helicopter were making serious noise, which was a good thing since they would drown out the sound of the plasma torch.

On the other side of Stonehenge, Ms. Günerro was still talking to a ring of Curukians.

Magnus, Mac, and Ms. Günerro shuffled through the debris and across the deck. They stopped at the giant pile of clothes where Lucas was hiding. He could see the sparkles on Ms. Günerro's blue boots.

Astrid, Travis, and Hervé were in a conversation

with Agent Janssens when suddenly she turned and approached the CEO of the Good Company.

Lucas listened closely.

"Ms. Günerro," the agent said, almost yelling above the noise. "Everyone at Interpol appreciates the support you give to all our various international charities."

"You're very welcome," Ms. Günerro said. "Being good just comes naturally to me."

The agent turned her attention to Magnus. "I have just one tiny problem remaining. . . ."

Magnus nodded impatiently. "What about?"

"It's all right, Chuckie," Ms. Günerro said. "I wanted an agent from Interpol here so that when we take our container, it would clearly show that the Good Company followed the rule of international law."

Ms. Günerro tipped her sunglasses down and looked over the top. "Agent Janssens, please continue. I love those boots, by the way."

Agent Janssens blushed. "Thank you," she said. "I got them in Rome." She cleared her throat. "The problem is that I sent out a bulletin about Lucas Benes."

What about him?" Magnus said.

Agent Janssens said, "These children on board tell me that Lucas went overboard during the night."

Ms. Günerro gasped, her hands covering her mouth. "That's a tragedy," she said. "I'm so sorry to hear this news."

Magnus folded his arms. "What exactly is the

problem for us?"

"If Lucas is wanted by Interpol and his body shows up in the Mediterranean, it's going to be awfully—"

"Fishy," Ms. Günerro finished.

"Yes."

"But that's really not my concern anymore," Ms. Günerro said. "If my container is on this ship, then I don't care about pressing charges against the Benes boy."

"If you're not pressing charges," Agent Janssens said, "I'll pull his name from the wanted list."

Lucas crawled backward out of his clothing cave to check on Alister's work. On the bottom of the phi container there was a perfect black gash gouged through about half of one side. The air smelled of burning metal. Through the welder's helmet Alister glanced up at Lucas, and then he went straight back to slicing the container.

Lucas crawled back to his nest and scooted on his belly right into the middle of the pile of clothes.

Astrid put her hands on her hips.

"Lucas hates dark water," she yelled. "He would have never in a million years jumped into the sea at night."

Travis asked, "Did you throw him overboard, Mac?"

Mac stepped forward. "We just told you that Lucas probably took one of the lifeboats."

"Aye," Eye Patch said. "No worries. He's with the celebrities over in Mallorca."

The Curukians moved closer, and Astrid and Travis backed up.

"My brother is floating somewhere out there in the Mediterranean Sea," Astrid said.

"Lucas is no longer wanted by Interpol," Agent Janssens said.

Travis said, "You're a police officer, aren't you?"

"Yes," Agent Janssens said. "But the fact that Ms. Günerro is not pressing charges against Lucas for wrecking her bus means I can no longer pursue him."

"Look at it this way," Ms. Günerro said. "The good thing is that Lucas is not wanted by the police anymore!"

"He could be dead," Travis said.

Astrid pointed her finger at Agent Janssens. "You just drop everything because Ms. Günerro says she cares more about her diamond container than she does my brother."

"I don't have to be right," Agent Janssens said. "I just have to follow the rules."

"Don't worry about this little ninny," Ms. Günerro said. "She will find an argument anywhere at any time, won't you, young lady? Don't answer that! I'm here for my container, so let's get on with it."

Ms. Günerro looked up at the mountain of containers in front of her. "Which one is mine?"

Mac offered his arm to her. With his other hand he

pointed. "It's on the other side of these containers."

"Well, you know," Ms. Günerro said, "it strangely resembles Stonehenge. Is the container ready to go, Mac?"

"Yes it is," he said, motioning to the others to get ready.

The Chinook moved into position with the hoisting wires dangling down.

Lucas backed out of the clothes pile and crawled over to Alister to check his progress. He had already started on the third side, but the bottom section of the container still appeared to be intact.

Alister kept the flame in his right hand and flipped the visor up with his left. The two dots on his cheeks were big and bright red.

"Five more minutes," Alister said. He flipped the visor down and continued melting away the old metal.

Farther back down the side of the ship, Kerala and Jackknife were cutting the Curukian boat free.

Lucas slid back under the Stonehenge containers and wormed his way through the laundry pile.

Astrid spoke up. "Why wouldn't you just leave the container here on the ship?"

Ms. Günerro turned around and faced Astrid. "What?"

"Yeah," Astrid said. "Just pick up the container at the port in Barcelona?"

"I know this game, young lady," said Ms. Günerro. "That's exactly what you want me to do. Send the container to Barcelona. Right? You're trying to pretend that the opposite of the opposite is not the opposite, right?"

"Exactly."

"The fact that you're trying to stop me is proof that I should take the container now because I'm sure you and your little friends have some plan waiting over there in the port. Only a fool would let it go to the port as planned."

Ms. Günerro turned her back on Travis and Astrid and Agent Janssens. She faced Magnus, Mac, and the Curukians.

Four boys stood at attention holding the four cables that were attached to the phi container.

"Enough!" Ms. Günerro said, "Hook this thing up to the helicopter and send it to our warehouse in Barcelona. Now!"

BYE-BYE PHI

Lucas slithered backward out of the pile of clothes. He flung a pair of underwear off his shoulder and ran his index finger across his throat to signal Alister. Jackknife shut down the generator while Alister killed the flame on the torch.

"Sorry," Alister said. "I could only get half of it cut. Ms. Günerro may lose a little, but she'll get away with the bulk of whatever is in there."

Lucas thought for a second. "But it'll bend, right?" he asked.

"After twelve years on the ocean, in the salt air," Alister said, "and half of the bottom cut—yeah, the metal should be pretty weak."

Lucas mashed his cap down. He needed to keep the Curukian disguise just a few minutes longer. He snatched up a rope and hitched it to the lip underneath the phi container. Then he dragged the other end of the rope to the bow and tied it to the ship's railing.

Mac and the Curukians were still trying to catch the helicopter's swaying cables.

As he slipped back behind Stonehenge, Lucas hoped his rope idea would work.

The helicopter moved into position. Its nose dipped, causing the hoisting wires to swing out over the bow again. The Curukians snatched them and clipped the hooks to the cables that were already on the phi container.

The container jolted as it lifted off the ship's deck. It tilted away from the opening that Alister had cut in the bottom. A rumbling sound came from inside the metal box. As the container rose, it swung and clunked into the surrounding containers. The cables holding it began to spin and straighten.

Lucas's rope, the one that was tied to the container and the railing, snaked across the deck.

Slowly the container rose and floated toward Mac's desk. Everyone was watching.

The helicopter would soon rip the railing off, but the rope would slow the helicopter for a minute. Long enough for Lucas to play one more game.

More slack came out of Lucas's line.

Just as the Chinook was starting to fly out over the water, Lucas's rope on the ship's railing became taut, and the helicopter and the railing played tug-of-war with the container in the middle. At this first sign of tension, one of the two cables that Lucas had unlocked popped loose.

The helicopter stopped its ascent and came back down a little.

A few diamonds sprinkled out of the opening that Alister had cut.

Ms. Günerro didn't move except for her eyes, which bulged as she watched the shiny stones peppering the deck like hail.

The helicopter jerked the container back and forth, up and down. Lucas's rope held tight.

As the midair battle for the container grew more violent, Lucas's rope yanked wildly on the container, whipping around and spinning the container like a giant piñata filled with diamond candy.

The second cable that Lucas had unlocked snapped free. The container dipped toward the gash Alister had cut, and more diamonds clattered out onto the deck.

A few Curukians tried sweeping them up with their hands.

Magnus and Ms. Günerro watched in horror, their mouths widening. Magnus pointed at the railing.

A group of Curukians stormed the bow and tried to unknot Lucas's rope, which only made the container swing more wildly. The helicopter stopped moving forward and hovered in place.

Magnus was on his walkie-talkie. "Tell the pilot to get out of here."

As the helicopter rose, the gash that Alister had cut began to wrench open like a giant mouth.

The container now spun out of control, swirling in wide loops above the ship. The container spat out diamonds, some of them rattling on the ship's deck but most spraying out into the sea. Gold coins pinged on the metal floor and rolled across the deck and into the water.

Fragments of rotted paper blew out across the ship like confetti.

The helicopter seemed to lose control and spun the container in wide and uneven arcs. It sailed over the water and back over the edge of the ship, where the container opened completely. Elephant tusks heaved out and smashed down on the deck and bounced into the water.

Everyone scattered.

The helicopter rose, snapping the railing from the ship's deck. With the lopsided weight beneath it, the helicopter itself began to spin out of control.

The Chinook crew released the cables so that the spinning container and the railing careened down toward the deck. It looked like it was going to smash right on top of everyone, but the container sailed above the ship and out over the water.

Then the metal box and all its remaining contents crashed into the sea. The water burbled around the sides of the phi container, and in moments it sank.

The helicopter tilted forward and flew away.

No one on board the ship said anything. Everyone stared at the wreckage.

Strewn all over the deck in front of them were maybe a million dollars in gold coins, diamonds, and a few ivory tusks. Sinking into the sea behind them was a fortune.

"My ivory!" Ms. Günerro screeched at the clump of Curukians. "My diamonds! You just ruined my entire shipment. My own boys destroyed ninety percent of the contents of that container!"

Just then a thin-armed Curukian came running up to the group gathered on the deck.

"Hey, two of our boats are missing," he reported.

"What do you mean?" Magnus asked.

"Someone cut the ropes," the boy said. "There're only two boats left."

"Maybe they floated away," Mac said.

"No," Ms. Günerro said. She stomped her boot and looked up to the sky. "No, there is only one way this got messed up. Lucas Benes is on this ship. Find him now!"

HOME IS WHERE THE HOTEL IS

Magnus ordered the Curukians, "Cut the other two boats free, first. I don't want Lucas to have an escape."

No one had noticed Lucas yet. He clumped in with the group of Curukians that was supposed to be looking for him. They walked straight across the deck past Ms. Günerro and Agent Janssens.

When he passed Astrid and the others, Lucas motioned for them to follow him. As soon as Lucas rounded the container with the surfboards, he huddled together with the other New Resistance kids.

"Out of the frying pan," Astrid said, "and into the fire."

"I know," Lucas said.

"There are too many to deal with," Travis said.

"What are we going to do?" Alister said. "Retreat?"

Jackknife said, "We're on an anchored drone ship."

Kerala added, "It won't take long for them to recognize Lucas."

Jackknife asked, "What about the Curukians' boats?"

"Magnus just cut them free," Astrid said.

Hervé stepped out from behind a container. "We are in the Mediterranean, no?" he said. He tapped his cane on the container with the surfing gear. "Why not take kite boards?"

It was a brilliant idea. If it could work.

With Magnus and most of the Curukians now on the other side of the ship, the New Resistance set out.

Hervé joined Lucas, Kerala, Travis, Jackknife, Astrid, and Alister as they each snatched a kite board from the container.

In a matter of minutes they were standing at the gap in the ship's railing. They tossed the boards down into the water and then launched their kites and jumped into the Mediterranean.

Holding on to the kite lines, they body-dragged a safe distance away from the ship. Then they locked their feet into the boards. Even Hervé with his cane and bum leg managed to get up and hang on.

The seven kids sailed away from the *Leviathan* and into shallow water. Behind them they could hear Ms. Günerro and Magnus and the Curukians yelling after them. Lucas looked back and saw Ms. Günerro putting on goggles and a snorkel. Two Curukians jumped into the water, but they dog-paddled and would never catch up.

Toward the south the two Curukian dinghies that Magnus had cut loose floated aimlessly.

The wind blew and the kites filled with air. Most of the kids just sailed straight to the shore. Jackknife of course did flips and tricks at every opportunity.

When they landed on the beach, the tide was

coming in and washing away sandcastles that had been built that day. They dropped the kites and sat on their boards and looked out over the water.

They were all pretty tired, but when Jackknife finally skidded his kite board onto the sand, he summed it up for everyone.

"That my friends," he said, "was awesome!"

The news of the container accident must have traveled fast. Groups of boats filled with scuba divers were speeding toward the newest and richest dive site on the Spanish coast.

A little while later they heard a familiar voice.

"Vámanos!" it said.

Wearing shorts and flip-flops and a flowery hat, Coach Creed marched across the beach.

"Where are we going?" Travis asked.

"To the hotel," Coach Creed said.

Jackknife asked, "Where is everyone from the plane?"

"They're at the hotel in Barcelona," Coach said. "Everybody from hotel school is coming here."

"Why?" Astrid asked.

"We had a problem with our concrete," Coach said. "The construction company that was doing work on the hotel in Las Vegas was paid off by the Good Company. They implanted audio and video equipment in the new dorms. It's a mess."

Astrid asked, "So what are we going to do?"

"We're moving to Spain."

Coach Creed drove them in a van from the beach to the Globe Hotel Barcelona where Mr. Benes, and the other New Resistance kids from the airplane were waiting. There they ate squid and octopus for dinner and slept four to a room. Lucas got the spot closest to the air conditioner so he wouldn't have to hear Jack-knife snore.

Lying in his bed in the Barcelona hotel, Lucas felt connected, somehow tethered to his past. To his mother, his grandfather, and his family's history. Knowing something about where he had come from gave Lucas new hope about where he was headed.

One thing he knew for certain: He would not stop until the Good Company was gone for good.

A CALL TO ACTION

Do the write thing.
Write a review online!

www.bit.ly/crimetravelers

Visit www.crimetravelers.com for information on speech & Skype requests.

If you've read this far in the series, I'd *really* love to hear your thoughts in an online review.
www.bit.ly/crimetravelers

Get Crime Travelers Book 3: Priceless

Lucas Benes faces his greatest challenge yet when he finds a secret message from his mother hidden inside a sunken cargo container.

In a near-death scuba diving experience, Lucas and the New Resistance kids learn that Good Company CEO Siba Günerro—along with her newest and most beautiful Curukians—is planning a massive art heist.

Lucas and friends scour the Spanish countryside looking for clues. But to unravel the mysteries of both the robbery and the cryptic message, Lucas must first discover the only thing that is worth more than priceless.

www.bit.ly/crimetravelers

MORE PRAISE FOR CRIME TRAVELERS

I read all my reviews and I would love to read yours! Here are some examples from literary magazines, newspapers, and publishing periodicals. They are merged here with reviews from parents, teachers, and kids to give each comment equal weight.

"Hilarious . . . An endlessly clever action-adventure."
"An exhilarating ride . . . a welcome addition to any library."
"Perfectly-sized chapters serve as success points for the middle grade reader."
"If you liked the Alex Rider series and are looking for something in the same vein, Crime Travelers is for you!"
"Kids who love spy action adventure stories will love this series."
"This story is like a 3-D movie in your head that keeps popping out every moment."
"As a middle school educator, I particularly appreciate how math helps Lucas and his team escape danger at every corner."
"Kids from ten on up should relish its campy flavor of excitement and thrills."
"Perfect for preteens and early teens who envision days of action and excitement."
"This was an excellent book, comparable to the likes of Alex Rider and The Hunger Games. The author fully enthralls the reader with a well-written book, satisfying to any spy-novel fan. I would recommend it for ages ten to fourteen."
"Reads like a movie script."
"It's good, clean fun."
Add your review here: www.bit.ly/crimetravelers.

Made in the USA
Las Vegas, NV
06 May 2021